DEPRAVED

DEPRAVED

FACES OF EVIL

DEBRA WEBB

PINK
HOUSE
PRESS

This book is dedicated to a very special angel, Samantha Nicole Custer. "May you always swim with the dolphins and fly with the butterflies!"

There are so many people I need to thank. First and foremost, my relentless and fearless editor Marijane Diodati, and all the amazing members of my street team who are too numerous to mention. I absolutely do not know how I would have done this without you. You continue to be my rock and my heart. May we rock on for many years to come! Finally, I want to thank my loyal readers. You continue to make my dream of storytelling come true.

"Original sin, therefore, appears to be a hereditary depravity and corruption of our nature, diffused through all the parts of the soul…"
John Calvin

CHAPTER ONE

Deputy Chief Jess Harris was furious…and just a tiny bit terrified. "You can't drive any faster, Lieutenant?"

Clint Hayes merged into traffic on I-20 West headed toward Birmingham proper before glancing at her, frustration sparking in his dark eyes. "Since I don't have a specific address, I can't see how breaking the speed limit will get us there any faster."

Another rush of fury tilted the maddening battle of emotions tugging at Jess. Rather than argue with him, she reached for her cell and tried Dan's number again. Chief of Police Daniel Burnett's cell went straight to voicemail. The band of worry and fear wound a little tighter around her chest. Dan had called Hayes less than fifteen minutes ago and warned that serial killer Eric Spears had been trapped. The trouble was Dan had purposely left out the location to keep Jess away from the line of fire.

Spears, aka the Player, had tortured and murdered dozens of women. His obsession with Jess had

1

started months ago. For weeks he had been getting closer and closer to her, targeting people somehow related to her—some she hadn't even known existed until they became victims.

Was it possible Spears had finally made a mistake?

For more than five years, the Federal Bureau of Investigation had searched for the serial killer known as the Player. As a profiler at Quantico's Behavioral Analysis Unit, Jess had studied the Player's depraved work. She had helped build his profile. The truth was she'd gone far beyond developing the description and definition that painted a picture of the sort of monster he was. She'd crossed certain lines in a misguided attempt to find him. Imprudent or not, her efforts were the sole reason they had a name and a face to go with the profile of a serial killer who sat at the highest level of the evil scale.

Jess squeezed her eyes shut and shook her head. She was also the reason he'd been released from custody after being questioned. Many more had died because of her failure to tie him to the evidence she'd discovered.

Nearly two decades with the Bureau and she had taken a rookie risk. Spears wasn't the only one who'd grown obsessed. Her need to stop him had prompted her to break the rules, ultimately ending her career. She'd landed back in her hometown of Birmingham, Alabama, as a deputy chief assigned to the new Special Problems Unit, a hybrid major crimes division.

And Spears had followed her.

Dammit. She stared at her unnervingly quiet cell phone. Why wasn't someone giving her an update? Desperate to find out what was going on and where the hell it was happening, Jess tried the cells of the other three members of her team. The voicemails of Detective Lori Wells, Sergeant Chet Harper, and Officer Chad Cook echoed one after the other in her ear. Making one last ditch effort, she tried Buddy Corlew, an old friend and local PI, who apparently had located Spears. How he had managed the feat when a multi-agency task force hadn't been able to do more than narrow down the approximate vicinity of where Spears *might* be was beyond Jess. Like the others, Buddy's cell went straight to voicemail.

She wanted to scream. "You're certain Chief Burnett didn't give you some idea of where they were headed?"

Hayes kept his attention on the unhurried flow of traffic as if this were a leisurely Sunday afternoon drive. "We've been over this twice already."

"This is not the time to try my patience, Lieutenant."

"Chief Burnett said Corlew had Spears cornered and he needed backup," Hayes repeated. "Wells and Harper were already en route to provide that backup. Burnett didn't want you involved so he refused to give me the location. Since the op is off the grid, there's no one to call for details."

How could Buddy keep this from her? As if she didn't know. Along with Dan and her team, Buddy wanted to protect Jess from Spears. Another blast of

3

outrage pumped through her veins. If Spears had been found she should be there. She had her suspicions about why Dan hadn't called anyone else on the Joint Task Force. If there was any chance there was a leak, either in the BPD or the Bureau, Dan didn't want Spears getting a heads up.

This time, Dan was the one taking a huge risk. Spears had made his intentions toward Dan clear—he wanted him dead. This whole scenario could be nothing more than a way to get Dan where he wanted him. Dammit!

Jess had to do something. "They could be walking into a trap. I should call Chief Black."

Hayes shot her a look of disbelief. There was no love lost between Jess and Black and everyone on her team knew it. "And tell him what?"

Jess held her breath and counted to ten. If the man wasn't the only member of her team handy she would fire him right this instant. "You have a better idea, Lieutenant?"

Before Hayes could respond, the cell phone clutched in Jess's hand clanged that old-fashioned ringtone.

Sylvia calling.

A frown furrowed its way across Jess's forehead. Dr. Sylvia Baron was a good friend and the associate coroner of Jefferson County. Jess's frown deepened. Why would she be calling? Her younger sister, Nina, had gone missing. Had she been found? Jess's heart took a painful dip. She hoped the news wasn't bad.

"You have news about Nina?" Jess asked rather than bother with a greeting.

"No."

Somehow, Sylvia packed enough uncertainty and worry into that single syllable word for Jess to comprehend it was undeniably bad news. Or maybe it was the distinct sound of sirens wailing in the background.

"You've heard from Dan?" Jess braced for the worst.

"I haven't spoken to Dan. It's Chad, Jess. We're headed to the ER at UAB. You need to come. You need to come *now*."

Chad Cook was the youngest member of her SPU team. Jess hadn't been able to reach him last night or this morning, and then all hell had broken loose. Come to think of it, Hayes hadn't mentioned him in connection with the backup being provided to Buddy either.

A new kind of fear crawled up Jess's spine. "What happened?"

"He's lost a lot of blood..."

Jess latched on to the fact that Sylvia didn't use the past tense. "He's alive."

"Barely."

"I'm on my way." She and Hayes were less than half an hour out.

"He was damned lucky, Jess. Another two or three minutes and he would've bled out. It's..." Sylvia's voice broke. "It's like the *others*. We're at the ER. I have to go."

The call ended. There was no reason for Sylvia to explain further. Jess understood perfectly what she meant.

Spears had done this.

UNIVERSITY OF ALABAMA AT
BIRMINGHAM HOSPITAL. 11:30 A.M.

Jess paced the small waiting room. Cook had been taken into surgery before she and Hayes arrived. She wished she had been able to see him. There were things she would have liked to say, starting with I'm sorry. She had asked for Cook to be moved to her team after he helped in the first case she'd worked with the Birmingham Police Department. Now he was fighting for his life.

She stalled in the middle of the small room and focused on calming her runaway heart. Chad Cook was twenty-three years old. He had his whole life ahead of him. He didn't deserve to die just because this sociopath wanted to get to Jess. Too many people had died for that reason already. With every fiber of her being she wanted to stop this son of a bitch.

She should have stopped him before now. What he wanted was no mystery. He wanted Jess. She was to be the final act in his sadistic game.

Jess's hand went to her belly. The situation was even more complicated now. Decisions about her personal safety were no longer just about her. The child she carried had to be protected. Her mind still reeled at the idea that she was pregnant. The concept had taken some adjusting to and, surprisingly, she had come to realize that this was what she wanted more than anything. She and Dan had waited a very long time for the wedding they were planning and to have a family.

Her heart squeezed as her thoughts went once more to Dan and her team. Was it possible that Spears had actually been found? Could this nightmare really be nearing an end? She stared at the phone she still held in her hand and willed it to ring.

The waiting room door opened and Sylvia walked in. The sleek lavender sheath she wore bore the crimson stains of her attempts to stop Cook from bleeding out. Their gazes met and pain twisted with a vengeance inside Jess. *Please, God, don't let him die.*

"How is he?"

"He's holding on."

Sylvia's words were hollow. The usually unflappable ME looked ready to fall apart. The dark circles under her eyes were evidence of how little sleep she'd had. Her sister had been missing for at least twenty-four hours. No one knew better than Jess that every passing hour lessened the likelihood of her being found alive.

Especially if Spears was involved.

Jess took Sylvia by the arm and guided her to the small grouping of chairs in the center of the room. "I know this is difficult." Sylvia and Cook had been intimately involved for a while now. Though Jess wasn't sure the relationship could be called anything more than friends with benefits, the terms were irrelevant at a time like this. "I need as many of the details as you can recall from the scene."

"I called him several times this morning." Sylvia's face pinched. "I hadn't spoken to him since Nina... since yesterday. He'd said he was coming to help." She shook her head and batted her eyelids to hold back the emotion shining in her eyes. "He never showed up. I assumed he was needed at work." A weary shrug lifted her shoulders. "I was too focused on the search for Nina to think about him again until this morning."

Jess hugged her. This was the first time she had seen the tough as nails ME so shaken. Nina was Sylvia's only sibling and she suffered from serious mental health issues. She'd disappeared from a prestigious private facility. In Jess's opinion, there was no question about Spears involvement. Nina was Dan's ex-wife and that made her a target. Another of Dan's exes had been murdered just days ago. Though they hadn't been able to make a connection between Meredith Dority's death and Spears, Jess sensed he was responsible. She suspected all of this, as well as the crash and burn of Dan's career, had been orchestrated to some degree by Eric Spears.

Sylvia inhaled a deep, bolstering breath. "I was headed to the office this morning to sign off on a couple of reports and it hit me that I hadn't heard from Chad. I changed course and dropped by his place."

Sylvia lapsed into silence. The woman was no doubt running on nothing more than adrenaline. Jess knew that routine all too well.

"I knocked several times, but he didn't answer. His car was outside and his dogs were barking." She shrugged. "I decided he was in the shower. When I started to unlock the door I realized it wasn't locked. I opened the door and called his name, but he didn't answer so I went inside." She closed her eyes for a moment. "The smell of blood was thick in the air."

"Any signs of a struggle?"

Sylvia shook her head. "None. He was just sitting on the floor, propped against the sofa as if he'd been watching television. Blood…was pooled around him."

Jess had made the call to secure the scene right after she'd spoken to Sylvia. Ensuring his dogs were taken some place safe was next on her list.

"On the way here," Sylvia went on, "I noted multiple bruises and ligature marks that were hours old." She moistened her lips. "Apparently after beating Chad, the bastard tied a tourniquet around his right thigh. He freed Chad's right hand so he could hold the tourniquet himself, then he sliced into the femoral artery and left Chad to die." Sylvia cleared her throat. "I'm guessing by the sheer volume of blood on the floor that Chad struggled with the tourniquet for an extended period." She pressed a hand to her throat. "I honestly don't know how he's still alive."

Jess gave her friend's hand a squeeze. "You saved his life."

Sylvia swiped at a tear that slipped past her firm hold on her emotions. "I should have checked on him sooner."

"You checked on him as soon as you could," Jess reminded her. "He's damned lucky you did." Dread knotted in her belly. "I should call his parents."

"I called his mother as soon as they took him into surgery." Sylvia grabbed a tissue from the box on the table next to her. "His parents should be here any minute."

"Can I call anyone for you?" Sylvia's family didn't need to wonder where she was. They were overwhelmed already.

A few feet away Hayes answered his cell. Jess hoped it was news from Dan. As soon as she learned where he was she intended to drive straight there and give him a piece of her mind. How could he leave her in the dark like this? What had he been thinking?

That he wanted to protect their child. Still, that was no excuse to leave her out of the loop completely. *Except he knows you too well, Jess.*

Sylvia managed a faint smile. "No. Thank you. I should call Daddy and see if there's news on Nina."

"Let me know if you need me," Jess urged as they both rose from their seats. With the Spears situation escalating, she felt way behind the curve on everything else going on around her, including the search for Nina.

"I will. Thank you."

Sylvia stepped away to make her call. Standing alone in the middle of the room Jess felt suddenly powerless. For nearly twenty years she had studied the faces of evil and learned that motive was the key to finding and stopping predators like Spears. Yet, all that knowledge and experience seemed utterly useless when it came to him. He was brilliant and possessed endless resources that made finding him like chasing a ghost. How did you stop a man who made no mistakes and who could disappear any time he liked?

Hayes appeared next to her. "Chief Burnett called. We have their location."

Anticipation charged through Jess, daring her to hope. "Spears?"

Hayes shook his head.

The hope bled out of her. "What about the hostages?" Spears had abducted four women in the past month. Rory Stinnett, Monica Atmore, Lisa Knowles, and the most recent victim who had not yet been identified. Four young women who, like Chad Cook, had their entire lives ahead of them.

"Three are in the house and they're alive."

Relief rushed through Jess, and then she frowned. "What about the fourth?"

Hayes shrugged. "She's not there."

Jess scrubbed at her forehead as she analyzed this news. "He takes one and leaves three behind... *alive?*"

"Why would he leave them alive?" Hayes asked the same question nagging at Jess.

The only possible answer had a smile stretching across her lips for the first time today. "Because he wasn't expecting company, Lieutenant."

Spears or someone in his close circle of followers had finally made a mistake.

CHAPTER TWO

669 ARGYLE DRIVE, 12:50 PM

BPD patrol units were everywhere. Jess doubted the residents of this exclusive neighborhood had seen this many cops at once anywhere except in old television footage of riots downtown. As Hayes passed through the official barricade at the end of the block, half a dozen reporters shouted questions at Jess.

"Looks like the operation is no longer off the grid," she noted, mostly to herself. Whatever had gone down here, Dan had a hell of a lot of explaining to do.

"No kidding." Hayes parked at the curb across the street from their destination.

Dan's car and Harper's SUV were farther up the block. Three ambulances were on the scene. Her pulse reacted. *For the hostages.*

On the lawn crime scene tape was being unreeled to warn the world that something evil had touched this place. The thick humidity in the air seemed to seep through her clothes as she emerged from the car. The Red Mountain neighborhood was eerily quiet, no matter that Birmingham's finest were now crawling around like ants at a picnic. Jess gazed at the house Eric Spears had used as his home.

Had he been here all this time?

Like the others along this highly sought after street, the home was more in keeping with the term mansion than house. Massive and ornate, the Greek Revival architecture left no doubt that the owner had sophisticated tastes and the means to support his opulent lifestyle.

As she and Hayes crossed the street the towering front door opened and Dan came out to meet her. Relief at seeing him unharmed temporarily over-rode her frustration with his decision to leave her out of the loop this morning.

"Crime scene techs are en route." Dan glanced toward the end of the street. "Harper and a team of officers are knocking on doors. We don't want Spears taking any other hostages or commandeer-ing another hiding place. Units are combing the streets for any sign of him."

"What about Gant and Black?"

Supervisory Special Agent Ralph Gant was Jess's former boss at the Bureau and the head of the Joint Task Force assigned to the Spears investigation. As acting chief of police, Harold Black would be show-ing up as well. Between Spears's efforts and those of Birmingham's mayor, Dan's career was sink-ing fast. Jess was the obvious motive. Her return to Birmingham had brought this trouble to Dan's door. He, of course, refused to see it that way. Daniel Burnett loved her and wanted her here no matter the cost to him.

"I spoke to Gant. He's on his way. I left a message with Sheila since Harold isn't in the office and he's not answering his cell."

"I guess he's going to miss the party. Lieutenant," Jess turned to Hayes, "track down Sergeant Harper and give him a hand, would you?"

"Yes, ma'am."

When Hayes was gone, Jess raised the issue that made her sick to her stomach. "Technically," she wished there was some other way to put this, "you and Buddy aren't supposed to be here."

Dan was on administrative leave and Buddy Corlew was a private citizen. There could be all kinds of complications related to evidence tampering or just plain old crime scene contamination going forward. Spears had a whole team of hotshot attorneys at his beck and call. She'd been down that road with him before. Then again, this time hostages had been left behind. Let his attorneys try dismissing that glaring fact.

"You let me worry about that." Despite the strength in his words, the defeat on Dan's face cut like a knife.

This was so damned unfair. "All right." She exchanged her sunglasses for the eyeglasses that were the bane of her existence. One of the fringe benefits of being over forty. "Tell me about what's going on inside."

"The house is clear," Dan said as they climbed the front steps. "Aside from the hidden basement level room where the hostages were being held, the place is practically empty."

At the door they paused and donned the necessary gloves and shoe covers before going inside. The entry hall was enormous and stark. Cold marble floors and cool white walls lent a mausoleum feel to the space. A side table was the only piece of furniture and it looked abandoned there with no rug beneath it or keys lying on its sleek top.

"Detective Wells is downstairs with the hostages and the paramedics."

"I'd like to speak to the hostages first." Jess needed to see with her own two eyes that the women were okay before she had a look around. Spears had left a survivor once and only then because he'd wanted her to live long enough to do one more thing for him. Amanda Brownfield had been as much his victim as his follower. Now she was dead, leaving her four-year-old daughter Maddie an orphan. Jess shivered at the memory.

The feel of Dan's hand at the small of her back was reassuring, yet each step forward echoed with a reminder that Spears had walked this same path. Had breathed this same air. The sensation that, even now, he was somehow watching made Jess tremble inside.

After passing several rooms flanking the hall they arrived at the kitchen. The room was huge and well equipped enough to have belonged in an upscale restaurant.

"Chad Cook is having emergency surgery," Jess had the presence of mind to say. She should have told Dan as soon as she arrived. Another indication of how shaken she was. *Pull it together.*

"What happened?" Dan looked as startled as Jess had felt when she'd heard the news.

"Spears or one of his followers left him for dead early this morning. Sylvia found him."

"Jesus Christ." Dan's eyes clouded with concern. "Is he going to make it?"

Jess swallowed at the thick lump of emotion welling in her throat. "Hope so."

"How's Sylvia holding up?"

"She looked exhausted."

Dan didn't have to say more for Jess to know he was thinking the same thing she was—this had to end.

Beyond the kitchen's center island an opening in a wall of gleaming white cabinetry exposed a staircase. Jess looked to Dan for an explanation.

"I think the house had a secluded wine cellar. Spears turned it into a torture chamber. We found the hostages naked and in glass cages. All three were obviously tortured."

"Right under our noses." Jess shook her head. How could he have been so close all this time?

Saving that infuriating question for later, she moved into the narrow space and descended the stairs. Several stainless steel tables and glass enclosures that looked a bit like freestanding show-ers filled the space. Next to the empty glass enclo-sures Lori Wells spoke quietly to three women already loaded onto gurneys and ready for transport by the half dozen paramedics crowded around them.

Dan touched Jess's arm, drawing her attention to him. "I'm going back up to find Corlew. We'll wait outside now that you're here."

Jess nodded, then watched for a moment as he walked away. Dammit, it was just so wrong for Dan to be in this position.

A worry for another time. Jess took another sur-vey of the room, noting the drains in the tile floor and the table filled with the instruments of torture the Player liked using on his victims. Her attention settled on the women as she crossed the room. Beautiful young women with long dark hair, just the way Spears liked them.

Lori spotted Jess and made her way toward her. "Paramedics have completed their assess-ments and started IVs. All three show signs of moderate dehydration. Lots of minor lacerations, some healed and some new, along with numer-ous bruises. I noticed visible indications of sexual assault," she said a little more quietly. "They're a little worried about Stinnett's BP and heart rate. She appears malnourished and isn't as responsive as the others."

Two of the paramedics headed for the stairs with the gurney carrying Stinnett. As much as Jess wanted to question her since she had been with Spears the longest, whatever medical attention she needed came first.

"I'd like you to oversee transport and let's get uniforms assigned to each of these women. I don't want them left alone for a second."

"I'm on it," Lori assured her.

Jess touched Lori's arm, stopping her before she got away. "I just came from the hospital. Cook's in surgery fighting for his life. He had an unexpected visitor this morning, but he was a lot luckier than the other victims we've seen this week."

Lori paled, understanding all too well what Jess's words meant.

In the last seven days three people had been murdered using the same MO as the attack on Cook. It was a miracle he had survived and Jess was immensely grateful he had. Losing a member of the team was unacceptable.

"I'll see if I can get an update on his condition."

Jess gave her a nod before shifting her attention to the two women she hoped would provide some clue as to where Spears might be going. "I'd like to ask a few questions, Mr. Reynolds," she said to the nearest paramedic whose nametag was visible.

"Make it fast, Chief. We need to roll."

"Thank you." Jess stepped closer to the two gurneys. A few feet away were the glass boxes where the hostages had been held. Jess counted six of those peculiar glass cages. Spears had intended to finish his game right here. He always took six victims. *She* was supposed to have been number six this time.

This is where it began, Jess, and this is where it will end.

Spears had taunted her with how this game would end, suggesting that her life had begun here—in Alabama—and it would end here.

Now suddenly his well-planned game had taken an unexpected turn.

You will lose this time, Spears.

Jess summoned the most reassuring face she could muster for the women who had escaped certain death. "I'm Deputy Chief Harris. I know you want out of this vile place, but I need to ask you a few questions before you're taken to the hospital."

Monica Atmore and Lisa Knowles stared blankly at Jess. She knew all too well the horror and violence they had suffered, and still it was more than evident to Jess that Spears had not given them the full treatment. Eric Spears loved wielding control and inflicting pain. Torturing others was the way he derived pleasure. Though he always murdered his victims, it was the torture that sated his depraved sexual desires. Jess doubted these women understood how very lucky they were.

She set her bag on the floor and gathered her notepad and pencil. "Were there any other hostages here with you at anytime since your arrival?"

If not here, where else would he have taken his latest victim? The pattern was the same each time a hostage was abducted. Spears delivered a photo to Jess and the Joint Task Force was left scrambling to solve the puzzle of the victim's identity. Jess opened the camera roll on her phone and showed the women the photo of the latest victim.

Monica Atmore nodded. "She…" Monica cleared her throat and sent a fleeting glance at Knowles. "She was here." Her lips quivered. "Is she still alive?"

"We hope so, but we haven't found her." Jess noted the needle marks on Atmore's arm. The Player drugged his victims. He kept them disabled to prevent resistance, but not enough to mask the intense pain he inflicted. "We believe he may have taken her with him. Can you tell me her name?"

"Presley Campbell," Lisa Knowles spoke up. "She's a grad student from Auburn. He took her out of her cage to…" She moistened her lips. "To *play* with her. She was crying and screaming. Then he suddenly stopped and turned out the lights. A while later when the lights came on again, the police were here and Presley was gone."

"Thank you, Lisa. Knowing her name will help. Was Presley wearing clothes when you last saw her?"

The women shook their heads. "He took our clothes as soon as we got here," Knowles said.

Jess studied each of the women for a moment. "What about this woman?" She showed them a photo of Nina Baron.

Both Knowles and Atmore shook their heads again.

Jess felt some sense of relief at learning Nina hadn't been in this torture room. Hopefully, that meant she wasn't with Spears. Still, with no ransom demand for the daughter of a wealthy United States Senator, Jess couldn't rule out his involvement.

"Was more than one person responsible for holding you here?" Jess asked.

Again, Knowles and Atmore looked at each other, but Knowles was the one to speak. "Just the one guy. He was tall with dark hair."

Her response prompted a new kind of tension. Jess thumbed through her camera roll again until she came to a photo of Spears. She displayed it first to Knowles and then to Atmore. "Do you recognize this man?"

Five endless seconds ticked off before Lisa spoke up. "I…" She shook her head. "I don't think so."

Jess showed them the photo again. "Please look closely."

Monica Atmore looked away. "I've never seen him before."

Unwilling to give up Jess chose a different tactic. "Anything at all you can remember could save Presley's life and help us stop the man who did this to you," Jess reminded them. "Did you at any time see what type of vehicle he used or any other person involved with your abduction? Were you taken anywhere else before or after coming here? Maybe you overheard a conversation or saw a visitor. The slightest detail might make all the difference."

The women stared at her as if she spoke a foreign language.

"Are you sure he isn't coming back?" Knowles glanced at Atmore, before going on. "He said we were going to die. Will he come after us again?"

"We will protect you, Lisa. You have my word, but the only way we can stop him permanently is if you help us."

"He's tall with dark hair." Knowles twisted her fingers together in her lap. "He brought us here and he hurt us."

Jess recognized a rehearsed answer when she heard one. As desperately as she needed real answers, she couldn't push any harder. These women were fragile and still felt vulnerable. "We almost got him today. That's why he was in such a rush and left you here. Do you understand that you're safe now?"

More of those endless seconds passed before one and then the other gave a negligible nod.

"I want you to think about my questions and I'll speak to you again soon. Right now, the paramedics will take you to the hospital and we'll notify your families that you're safe."

Before the paramedics could wheel her away, Atmore asked. "Are you Jess?"

Jess wasn't surprised they had heard her name. "I am."

"He did this to us because of you." Atmore's lips trembled. "All he wants is you."

Knowles stared at Jess, the same accusation in her eyes. It was true. They had suffered unimaginable horrors and pain because Eric Spears wanted to punish Jess.

"I'll see you again when you're rested." Jess gave the women a final nod before walking away. Every move Spears had made for the past two plus months had been about her, and he was still out there with at least one hostage.

Upstairs three forensic techs waited in the entry hall as Dan outlined the situation. When the group fanned out Jess moved toward the man she loved with all her heart. The urge to throw herself into his arms and let this dam of emotions pressing against her breastbone burst free was almost overwhelming.

Instead, she did what she had to do. She needed to go through this house and find some damned evidence that Eric Spears had been here. But first, she had to get Dan out of here before Black showed up. "Where's Buddy? I thought the two of you were going to wait outside."

"The Crime Scene Unit arrived and...there's something in the parlor you need to see."

Before she could question the concern in his eyes, the paramedics hurried past with Atmore and Knowles. Jess watched until they were out the front door. "They blame me, you know."

Dan reached out and caressed her cheek, his tender touch calming. "They'll see things differently when this is over."

Jess wasn't so sure. For Dan's sake she summoned her best attempt at a smile. "Probably so." She pushed aside the troubling thoughts for now. "What is it I need to see?"

"This way." As they reached the French doors separating the parlor from the hall, he hesitated. "Before we go in," worry carved deeper lines into his handsome face, "I need you to brace yourself for what Spears left behind in there."

Uncertainty tugged at Jess. "All right." A few minutes ago he'd basically told her there was nothing here.

Unlike the entry hall the parlor room was elegantly furnished with oversized leather sofas and upholstered side chairs. Crystal decanters filled with richly colored spirits waited on the bar. Across the room Buddy stood before the fireplace staring at a painting hanging over the mantel.

Even from a distance of fifteen feet or so the painting stole her breath.

All he wants is you.

Buddy said something, but the words didn't register. Jess could only stare as she moved closer to the fireplace. The painting was of her standing on a sidewalk. She couldn't quite pinpoint the location. The image was like looking in the mirror.

"Whoever painted this," Buddy said, "nailed it, kid. Damned thing is as lifelike as a photograph."

"We missed it the first time we went through since finding Spears and his hostages were the primary objectives," Dan explained.

"It was easy to miss," Buddy said. "He had it covered up." He gestured to the silky drape lying on the floor.

"As soon as the evidence techs are finished we'll have it removed," Dan promised.

Jess had to look away from yet another symbol of Spears's obsession with her. "There's nothing in the rest of the house?"

"One of the bedrooms is furnished," Buddy explained. "Expensive men's toiletries in the bathroom, even more expensive menswear in the closet. No personal items like jewelry, photos, or notes we could find."

"No sign Nina was held here?"

"None we found," Dan said, confirming what the women had stated.

"This is a big house," Jess countered. "Could you have missed something else?"

"It's possible," Dan admitted.

"Definitely," Buddy seconded.

Jess turned to Buddy, "Before we go any further, I want to know how you found this place?"

Buddy Corlew was Jess's oldest friend. A former BPD detective turned PI, he was the last person to visit Amanda Brownfield before her escape from the hospital. Acting Chief of Police Harold Black was convinced he had something to do with her escape and possibly her murder. Jess knew better. Spears had sprung Amanda. She'd told Jess as much when she called mere hours before her death. Be that as it may, Black was determined to take Buddy down.

"Amanda led me here."

Jess wanted to shake him. "Dammit, Buddy. You said you had nothing to do with her escape."

Buddy held up his hands surrender style. "I swear I had nothing to do with it."

"Then tell me how this happened."

"When I went to see her, she gave me nothing, like I told you. Just more of that ridiculous talk about Spears and questions about you. I figured she was either curious about you or digging for tidbits to give Spears."

Jess folded her arms over her chest. "And?"

"Before I left, she asked me to lean closer. I did and she kissed me—"

"Buddy," Jess cautioned, "get on with it."

"She whispered *one percent* in my ear. I didn't know what to make of it at first. After I chewed on it awhile, I decided it could be a license plate. I had a friend at the DMV look up variations of the phrase and the only one he came up with in the Birmingham area was 1PERCNT. The owner of that license plate lives across the street. I figure Amanda saw it when she was here."

Jess couldn't speak for a moment. Amanda had provided the only clue to Spears's where-abouts. As hard as she tried, Jess failed to conquer the shaking that started deep inside her. Amanda Brownfield had been a diagnosed psychopath. She had stolen the idyllic childhood Jess remembered in one fell swoop with claims that Jess's father was also her father. DNA had substantiated her claim. She and her ancestors had murdered dozens of people and buried them on their Jackson County farm. Yet, before facing death, Amanda had unearthed a kernel of goodness from somewhere deep inside her.

On the other hand, the lead Amanda gave Buddy could have been part of the plan all along, but Jess didn't think so. Eric Spears never left survivors. Lori Wells had survived an up-close encounter with Spears and his protégé Matthew Reed. In that instance, Reed had been the one to fail to end her life—not Spears. Amanda had met Spears and lived to tell about it, but only because Spears had one last task for her before he murdered her. With all that made her a cop, Jess believed finding these three women alive was *not* part of Spears's carefully laid plans.

"You staked out the place," Jess suggested when both men appeared to be waiting for her to speak next.

Buddy nodded. "Watched it night and day. A limo came and went this morning. The driver pulled into the garage but didn't close the door. That's when I got a visual on Spears. I saw him get out of the limo and go into the house through a side door in the garage."

"You never left your surveillance post once you spotted him?" The urge to tear this house apart was clawing at Jess. Spears could still be hiding in here somewhere.

"Not for a second."

"Then how did he get away?"

"I can't be certain he didn't slip out the back door before Dan and your crew got here, but once we surrounded the house, no one came out." Buddy hitched his head toward Dan. "All I know is he was gone when we got inside."

"Unless he was tipped off before we arrived and I don't see how that's possible since no one knew we were coming except you," Dan argued. "There has to be another way out. We just haven't found it yet."

Jess turned back to the fireplace and the unnerving painting above it. *Where the hell are you, Spears?* "I guess this painting didn't have as much sentimental value as he wanted us to believe considering he left it behind, too."

She desperately wished he had taken it and left the fourth victim. Then again, he had been in a hurry. Her cell chimed with an incoming text message. Jess dug around in her bag until she found it. Hopefully there was good news about Cook or Nina, maybe both.

Tormenter.

Her heart stumbled. "It's him." She swiped the screen to download the message.

It's only a painting, Jess. I'll have the real thing soon.

She spun around, surveying the room from floor to ceiling. "He's watching us or listening somehow."

Dan took the phone from her and read the message. "Son of a bitch."

They spread out, examining every inch of the room for monitoring devices. Silence thickened as their search grew more frantic and frustrating. Jess was just about to suggest they call Dan's friend who'd located the monitoring devices planted in his former home when shouting reverberated in the entry hall.

"Oh hell," Buddy grumbled.

"Where is Chief Harris?"

Jess clenched her teeth to hold back the answer she would have liked to give Acting Chief of Police Harold Black as he stormed into the parlor. His furious glare landed on her first.

"What's going on here?" he demanded. "I received a message from my secretary with this outlandish story. When I arrive, I see two of Spears's hostages being loaded into ambulances under the supervision of one of your detectives. What is this, Harris?" He surveyed the room, his attention falling at last on the portrait over the fireplace. His anger gave way to surprise. "God help us."

"Eric Spears has been residing in the house for several weeks now and no one noticed," Jess informed him. "He left behind *three* of his hostages— alive. I think maybe God already did his part. Now we're trying to do ours, that's what's going on here."

The fury glittered to life once more in Black's dark eyes. "I demand a full accounting of what has taken place here this morning!"

"This was my call, Harold," Dan announced.

Jess bit back a groan.

Black shifted his attention to Dan. "I see." He drew in a big breath, puffing out his chest. "I mean no disrespect, Dan, but I would urge you to stand down. You have no law enforcement authority at this time and any measures you have taken are a personal liability as well as a legal problem for this department."

Dan held up a hand. "Detectives Wells and Harper were the first on the scene. Every step taken here has been by the book, Harold."

"Attorneys representing Spears will have a field day with this," Black contended. "Where is the warrant? What is Corlew doing in here?" Black gestured to Buddy. "What were you thinking, Dan?"

Outrage lashed through Jess. "I, for one, suggest we get on with the business of finding a serial killer."

Black glared at her again. "You and I will discuss this in my office."

Jess glared right back at him. "The bottom line is Buddy Corlew discovered Spears's hiding place when no one else had. After a visual confirmation that Spears was in the house, he called my detectives to the scene. Considering God and everyone else knew Spears had hostages, exigent circumstances precluded the need for a warrant. And since time was unquestionably of the essence, Mr. Corlew provided what assistance he could as a private citizen. Any other questions, Chief?"

When Black couldn't seem to decide what to say to her tirade, Jess turned to Dan. "I'll see you later." Uninterested in wasting more time, she stepped around the acting chief of police and headed for the door.

"We are far from finished talking about this, Chief Harris," Black tossed at her back. "I will see you in my office."

Jess kept walking. "I'll check my calendar."

"Buddy Corlew," Black announced, "you'll be coming with me for questioning in the investigation of Amanda Brownfield's murder."

Jess hesitated at the door and sent Buddy a look she hoped relayed how sorry she was for all this. Black knew damn well Buddy hadn't killed Amanda. This was nothing more than an opportunity for him to show he was the boss. *For now.*

Her old friend gave her a lopsided grin before turning to Black and saying, "Always happy to oblige the BPD."

Dan caught up with Jess on the front steps. "Are you headed to the hospital?"

"I am. I want to check on Cook and follow up with the victims." What she would really love to do first was slap some sense into Harold Black. Thankfully, reason had overruled any such foolish act.

"Hayes and Harper are both needed here. I'll take you."

Jess stalled on the bottom step. Dan was damned worried about her and he already had more than his share of trouble weighing on those broad shoulders. Nina Baron had gone missing. Though she and Dan had been divorced for more than a decade, he still cared about Nina and her family. On top of that, his first wife, Meredith Dority, had been murdered just two days ago. He'd been placed on administrative leave from his position as chief of police after Meredith's murder. Between his visit with Meredith just before she died and evidence related to Captain

Ted Allen's disappearance turning up on his property, Dan was considered a person of interest in both cases. All that didn't even take into consideration that his home had burned to the ground a mere two weeks ago.

How could he possibly have room left to worry about her? Yet, somehow he did. He loved her. He loved the child she carried, *their* child.

Rather than argue with him about whether he was hovering and showing his overprotective side again, she smiled. "Thank you. I'd appreciate it."

Whatever else went wrong, holding tight to Dan was the right thing to do.

CHAPTER THREE

"He drugged me." Officer Chad Cook licked his dry lips before he continued. "I opened the door and he jammed the needle into my shoulder."

Jess could only imagine what went through Cook's mind at that moment. Unlike most of Spears's victims, he would have been well aware of how the encounter would likely end. He was alive and that was a flat out miracle. The surgeon had saved his leg, but Cook would be out of commission for some time. He would be in ICU for the next seven days and, barring any unforeseen issues, released a week or so later. There would be extensive physical therapy, and though the prognosis was optimistic, the final results were unclear at this time.

"Ketamine," Jess confirmed. "It works quickly. A high enough dosage can put down an elephant."

Cook laughed a dry, rusty sound. His throat was raw from the hours of intubation. With all the tubes and wires and the open incision required for healing after the extended period of compromised blood flow, he looked a mess and it broke Jess's heart.

"Spears's drug of choice," he said, his voice gravelly.

Lori smiled down at him. "Definitely not mine."

One corner of Cook's mouth curled. "Mine either."

Lori had been drugged with Ketamine part of the time she was held by Matthew Reed. She had suffered and seen things no cop wanted to experience. She and Cook were now part of a very small club—the Player's Survivors Club.

When his doorbell rang Cook had thought it was Sylvia. His cheeks had flushed with embarrassment as he'd explained that Dr. Baron sometimes stopped by his place before going to work in the mornings. He always ushered the dogs into his guest bedroom since Sylvia wasn't a big fan. Lucky for the dogs. Had they not been shut up in the extra bedroom they would, in all probability, have ended up casualties. The two loyal animals had almost clawed and chewed their way through the door by the time Sylvia arrived. The idea of having a dog around the house was growing on Jess.

"You got a good look at the man who attacked you," Jess said, easing the conversation back to where Cook left off.

"It was that guy who's been following you around. I recognized him immediately from your description. He was tall with dark hair." Cook coughed hard. When he'd caught his breath, he cleared his throat. "He wore Wayfarer sunglasses. Cost at least two hundred bucks." He coughed again.

The dark-haired man had been following Jess off and on for a month, more off than on lately.

"You need water." Lori filled the plastic cup from his bedside table, added a bendable straw, and held it to his lips. "Take it slow."

He swallowed several small sips. "Thanks. That's better." He looked to Jess and resumed his story. "I didn't lose consciousness at first, just kind of felt loopy and too weak to get up."

"Did he say anything that you recall? Did he use his cell phone?"

"He kept talking about how—excuse me, Chief—he got off on following you around. He said Amanda Brownfield was a practice run for what Spears wanted to do to you. He bragged about how he hoped he got to watch."

Jess banished the images of Amanda's battered and abused body. "At any time did you overhear the dark-haired man speaking to anyone else? Maybe when he thought you were unconscious?"

Cook frowned, and then flinched. Jess hated to push him like this. He'd only been out of recovery for forty-five minutes. He was still a little groggy and likely experiencing some degree of pain.

"Somebody—a male—said something like: *No more mistakes, North.* I can't say for sure if it was him or someone else. I was pretty much out of it after he dosed me up with that second hit of ketamine." He coughed and Lori offered him another drink, but he declined. "I might've dreamed it. I don't know for sure. That's the only other thing I remember until he was telling me I'd better stay awake if I wanted to live. Then he left."

"North." Jess mulled over the name. "This could be an important break. Good job, Cook."

Another of those fleeting smiles tugged at his lips. "Thanks, Chief. I tried real hard to stay awake so I could tell you to watch out for him."

More of that exasperating emotion she'd been dealing with all morning swelled in her chest. "We should go so you can rest. There will be two guards outside your room at all times."

"We've got you covered." Lori gave his hand a squeeze. "Chet's taking your dogs over to your mom's house so no worries, okay?"

Cook managed a faint nod. "No worries."

In the corridor, Jess reminded the officers on duty to notify her immediately if there was any change in Officer Cook's condition. Since Cook had still been in recovery when they first arrived, she and Lori had checked on Stinnett, Atmore, and Knowles. All were doing as well as could be expected and their families were on the way. Jess wished one of the women would break her silence about Spears. They were alive and that was what mattered. Still, any kind of lead could turn the tide on the investigation. Maybe tomorrow she would push one or all three a little harder.

Her cell phone vibrated, rattling against a Coke can she'd shoved into her bag between patient visits.

She'd silenced the nuisance before beginning the interviews. She fished it out and checked the screen. *Gant.*

"I was just thinking about you," Jess said in lieu of hello. "Officer Cook says the man who left him for dead mentioned a name. *North.* Does that ring a bell?" Both she and Gant had worked on the Player case for years.

"I'll have the name run through the databases," Gant said. "I'm in Birmingham. Chief Black picked me up at the airfield. I'll see you at Eighteenth Street in half an hour."

Jess wasn't surprised that Gant was here already. Not only was this the first time any of Spears's victims had been found alive, this was the first time they'd had even a clue where he'd kept the victims of one of his games. Two other women who'd been held with Rory Stinnett initially had been released alive, but followers of Spears had actually abducted those two as a sort of game preview.

Typically, the victims would disappear one per week until his annual killing spree was over. The bodies were always discovered at different locations and times with no evidence of where they had been prior to discovery. Locating the house Spears had used was, in fact, a huge break in the case. Just not the one they needed to find him, apparently.

"I'll be there." Jess ended the call and set her phone back to ring, then tossed it into her bag. "I guess there's a conference."

"Maybe they found something at the house that we missed this morning." Lori pressed the call button for the elevator.

"We can hope." Spears never made mistakes and he always had a fall back plan. He'd likely had a car stashed in the neighborhood for a hasty getaway. Yet, to take a hostage and run was not characteristic behavior. Spears had taken a huge risk.

"I sent Harper the name Cook remembered," Lori mentioned, "and asked him to see if he could find anything in our local databases."

"Good thinking." Jess could always count on her team to take the initiative. She hoped Cook would be able to come back to work when he had recovered. She didn't want to lose him.

Damn you, Spears.

FEDERAL BUREAU OF INVESTIGATION
FIELD OFFICE 18TH STREET, 5:40 P.M.

Harold Black droned on about what they hadn't found in the house on Argyle Drive. Jess held back her sighs, resisted the tapping of her toes, and strove for patience. She would very much like to get to the part about what they had discovered, which she anticipated would be nothing of significance.

Black finally sat down, confirming Jess's conclusion, and all eyes moved to the end of the conference table where Gant was seated. He glanced at his notes and leaned forward, bracing his elbows on the table. "For as long as it takes, a team of agents and detectives will continue work in the house in hopes of finding any overlooked piece of evidence as well as the route Spears used to escape."

"Assuming," Black cut in, "he was actually on the premises at the time of the rogue invasion by Chief Harris's team."

"We had exigent circumstances, Chief Black," Jess said with a feigned smile. "Looks like the decision was the right one since three victims were recovered from the scene. Alive, I might add."

"Three victims who haven't identified Spears as their abductor," he countered.

Gant held up a hand when Jess would have fired back. "As for the text message Spears sent Chief Harris, the entire house and property are monitored by cameras, easily accessed from any Wi-Fi device. Spears could have been watching from anywhere."

"Are you corroborating he was not in the house this morning?" Black did not intend to let it go.

"Actually," the woman seated to Gant's left spoke up, "we believe he was not only in the house, but that he was alerted via his state-of-the-art surveillance system that he had been found."

Jess didn't know the lady, but she liked her already.

"This is Special Agent Vicki Hancock," Gant explained. "She's new to BAU and the Spears case. She'll be staying in Birmingham for the duration."

Hancock presented a smile to all at the table. She looked to be about Jess's age. Well dressed. Dark blond hair. For her sake, Jess hoped they stopped

Spears soon. Otherwise, the agent might need to look at setting up permanent residence in the Magic City.

"What we can confirm about this morning's raid is that Spears was not expecting us," Gant said, echoing Jess's earlier conclusion. "He was caught off guard and anyone who has worked on the Player investigation can tell you that has never happened before. We're hoping a neighbor we haven't questioned as of yet will have seen him leave or noticed something out of the ordinary recently."

"Like the fact that he ran out of the house with a naked woman in tow," Jess reminded her former boss. Not at all a typical Spears getaway. Buddy had absolutely blindsided him. Spears had not anticipated that Amanda would betray him.

Gant sent her a look that warned she should stow the sarcasm. "The nearest traffic cams are well away from the exclusive neighborhood and haven't yielded any results as of half an hour ago."

"It's difficult to take advantage of traffic cams," Black interjected, "when we don't know the type of vehicle Spears is using. The black Infiniti believed to be used by one of his followers was not found in any of the footage covering this morning's traffic near the Red Mountain neighborhood."

"That's because the driver was busy trying to murder a member of my team," Jess reminded him.

Black ignored her while Gant asked for an update on Cook as well as the three women rescued from the scene. Lori provided the latest information from her point of contact at the hospital. Cook's condition had been officially upgraded from critical to stable.

"Where are we on determining whether or not Spears was involved with Nina Baron's disappearance?" Gant asked.

"Given her connection to Dan Burnett," Black spoke up before Jess could, "I believe we should treat her disappearance as if Spears ordered it. As for evidence, we have none at this time."

"None of the victims saw Nina and Spears hasn't contacted me about her," Jess added. "Usually, he takes great pleasure in keeping me informed of his exploits. That said, I agree with Chief Black. We should treat her disappearance as if she is one of his victims."

Agent Hancock briefed those seated around the table on the fourth victim, the one still missing. Presley Campbell, twenty-four, was a graduate student at Auburn University. She had been missing for seventy-two hours. Since she lived alone and her family was in Tupelo, Mississippi, no one had reported her missing. Everyone contacted was stunned to learn she had been abducted.

Between the BPD, Jefferson County Sheriff's Department, and the Bureau, the city was crawling with cops searching for Spears, Campbell, and Baron. Every single media outlet, even Facebook, was warning citizens to be on the lookout.

By the time the meeting ended Jess was ready to collapse. It had been one hell of a long day. As exhausted as she felt, she couldn't help wanting to go back to the Argyle Drive house and do some more poking around. Gant insisted he had the scene under control. Maybe tomorrow she'd drop by anyway.

Outside, Lori fired up her sassy red Mustang and pointed it toward the Forest Park neighborhood Jess called home for now. She'd rented the small apartment over George Louis's garage shortly after she returned to Birmingham. The apartment was small, but the historic neighborhood was nice and it was all she'd needed at the time. After the fire at Dan's house, he'd moved in with her. It was a little cramped, nevertheless, they were making the best of it. The house hunting had begun in earnest. With any luck they would decide on one soon.

Her life had changed dramatically in the past two and a half months. She'd walked away from a career two decades in the making with the Bureau. The man she'd fallen in love with at seventeen was now her fiancé and the father of the child she carried. Getting pregnant hadn't been part of the plan, for sure. Yet, she couldn't deny being a little excited about the prospect of motherhood. Who knew if she'd be any good at it since her sister appeared to have inherited all the nurturer genes. Jess was work oriented. She spent more hours at work than she did anywhere. If she were completely honest with herself she would admit that work had defined her until very recently.

Lately, she'd come to realize how important an existence beyond work was. There were so many things out of balance in her life right now—everything about her childhood had been turned upside down. The one thing she knew without doubt was that Dan loved her and she loved him.

And they were going to have a baby. As well as a house. And a dog.

Jess groaned. "I completely forgot about the dog. I hope Dan dropped by and let him out." Otherwise there would be a huge mess waiting for her at home.

Lori laughed. "It's difficult to have a pet when you keep a cop's hours."

Jess sagged in her seat. "I hope I'm better at making arrangements for my child than taking care of this puppy."

"My mother swears it comes naturally," Lori assured her.

"I sincerely hope so." The poor puppy! He'd showed up at Jess's door last week. So far her efforts to find his owner had proven futile. She had never owned a dog and really hadn't planned to own one now, but how did you drop a creature that cute at the pound?

She couldn't do it.

Lori parked in the driveway in front of Jess's apartment. The BPD cruiser assigned as her surveillance detail parked next to her. Since Dan's rental car wasn't at home, Jess suspected the dog had been inside without a break since early that morning. It was now seven o'clock.

"I'll walk you in and help you clean up," Lori offered.

Jess waved her off, and then reached for the door. "Go home. I spend my days slogging through murder scenes, how bad can it be in there?"

"If you're sure."

"Go," Jess repeated before closing the passenger side door.

"See you tomorrow!"

Jess waved a goodbye and slung her bag onto her shoulder. As soon as she cleaned up, she was going to have a long warm bath and a glass of milk with chocolate chip cookies. The sound of yapping stopped her at the bottom of the stairs leading up to her place. Before she could turn around a warm fuzzy body slammed into her legs.

"Puppy!" Jess glanced up at her apartment door to ensure it was closed. "How did you get out?"

"He must have sneaked out behind you this morning."

Jess smiled at George Louis, her landlord, as he strolled toward her. "I was sure I left him inside. I hope he wasn't any trouble."

"A little digging and nosing around in the flowers."

Jess cringed. "I'm sorry about that, George." This was the second time the puppy had gotten into his flowers. "Bad puppy," she scolded.

"It wasn't so much trouble." George adjusted his eyeglasses, and then clasped his hands behind him. "A few flowers to replace."

She couldn't help wondering if George had his fingers crossed behind his back. "I'll pay you for those," Jess insisted. What in the world was she going to do with this rambunctious puppy? How could she have a dog when she was never home?

"I've already taken care of the flowers. I won't have you think of it again."

Before she could protest, George went on, "I fed him at six. I had some homemade jerky he thoroughly enjoyed."

"Thank you, George." Jess ruffled the puppy's fur. "You're too kind."

"I should let you get upstairs. Have a nice evening, Jess."

"You, too."

George gave her a final wave and wandered toward his house. She'd started up the stairs when the sound of crunching gravel drew her attention. Dan was home. He shut off the engine and emerged from the BMW he'd rented. She smiled. The puppy barreled toward him.

"Hey there, boy." Dan scratched him behind the ears.

"We left the puppy out this morning." Jess felt terrible at the idea of having been so neglectful.

Dan frowned and kissed her on the cheek. "Are you sure?"

She nodded. "George took care of him."

Dan glanced toward the main house. "That was nice of him."

"Any word on Nina?" Jess asked as they climbed the stairs.

"Nothing yet. I spent some time with the Senator this afternoon. Everything that can be done is being done. At this point, all we can do is pray she's found unharmed. The longer she's off her meds the more paranoid and delusional she'll become. She could become psychotic and completely out of touch with reality."

Jess wished there was more she could do.

While Dan unlocked the door, she checked her phone. "I haven't heard from Buddy. I hope Black didn't arrest him." Of course Buddy was a person of interest in Amanda's death, but he was definitely not her murderer. In Jess's opinion Black was abusing his power where Buddy was concerned. Revenge, she supposed, for Buddy's years of trying to make the BPD look bad.

"Corlew was released about four this afternoon."

Jess waited until Dan had entered the security code so the alarm's infernal beeping would stop before she questioned his news. The puppy raced into the apartment ahead of them. "Did you talk to him?"

Dan shook his head. "I sent my attorney over to represent him. Black was ready to back off after Frank Teller made an appearance."

"You asked your attorney to help Buddy?" Talk about an about face. The rivalry between the two was legendary. It went all the way back to their days as competing quarterbacks in high school. "That was nice of you."

Dan shrugged. "It's not a big deal. It was more about showing up Harold than helping Corlew."

Even Dan was damned frustrated with Black right now and the two had been friends for years.

"How did the conference with Gant go?" Dan peeled off his jacket and tossed it on the sofa.

Jess started to rattle off her complaints about the Spears investigation, but she stopped herself. She was so glad to be home with Dan. All she wanted to do was stare at him—well, maybe there were other things she wanted to do as well. "I don't want to talk about work." She tossed her bag aside and put her arms around him. "We're home. I want to talk about us."

A smile widened that sexy mouth of his. "Do you have a fever?" He touched her forehead, then her cheek. "Should I call the doctor?"

She shook her head. "You can draw us a bath."

"Now that," Dan kissed her lips, "is what I call a nice welcome home."

Dan carried her to the bathroom and closed the door. "Have I told you today how beautiful you are, Jess? And how much I love you?"

Jess smiled. "You might have mentioned it."

With the puppy yapping his indignation and steamy water filling the tub, Dan stripped off her clothes. It felt as if a weight had been lifted from her, leaving her skin exposed to the vivid contrast of the cool air whispering from the air conditioning and the searing heat of his touch. He kissed every part of her that he bared. By the time he had ditched his clothes her thighs were trembling and her heart was racing.

He made love to her slowly, and then they bathed each other and made love again. Long minutes later, the water had cooled and she had melted against the warmth of his chest. She didn't care if they stayed in this tub all night.

What mattered was that they were together.

CHAPTER FOUR

Sergeant Chet Harper tapped the photo he'd printed and taped to the case board. "The security footage at Cook's apartment shows the dark-haired man entering the building at six-thirty yesterday morning and exiting at nine. Dr. Baron arrived at ten-twenty, followed by the paramedics at ten-forty."

Jess propped against the front of her desk and studied the timeline Harper had created. Her stomach clenched each time she thought of how close Chad Cook had come to dying. The only aspect of the past twenty-four hours that had provided any hope was the idea of how close they'd come to catching Spears.

All because Amanda Brownfield had given Buddy a clue.

Lori Wells walked to the board and picked up the Dry Erase marker. "Forensic techs have found no evidence."

"Spears and his followers never leave any," Hayes tossed in. He leaned back in his chair and propped his leather-clad feet on his desk. "And yet they don't seem to mind being captured on video."

Hayes had foregone a jacket, but the polo and slacks he'd chosen somehow looked elegant on him. Jess decided Hayes, like Dan, could make anything look good. She wondered if the lieutenant and Harper had finally decided to be friends since they both wore polo shirts minus jackets this Saturday morning. *Doubtful.* Jess wasn't sure the two men would ever fully trust each other. Maybe later she would ask Lori how things were going. Hayes was the newest member of the team. He was a damned good detective, but a little on the arrogant side, landing himself on probation with Jess.

"I think," Jess shifted her attention back to the conversation, "it's safe to assume they don't care because they already know their fate." She thought of Fergus Cagle, the Vance sisters, Richard Ellis, and then of Amanda Brownfield. All had given their lives to fulfill the desires of a sociopathic serial killer. How had Eric Spears risen to such power?

"Presley Campbell's parents arrived in Birmingham this morning," Lori mentioned. "Chief Black met them at the airport."

Jess resisted the impulse to make a nasty remark about Black enjoying the hell out of Dan's job. Dwelling on that travesty took far too much energy. All their efforts had to be focused on finding Presley Campbell alive and stopping Spears.

"Hopefully, we'll have something more than this," Jess stared at the case board, "to give them soon." She rubbed at her forehead and the headache pounding there. "What do we have on the name North?"

"This is where things take a turn for the better." Harper smiled and gestured to Lori.

Jess perked up. She could definitely use some good news.

"Quentin North, forty-four, Caucasian," Lori taped a new photo of the dark-haired man on the board, this one from the DMV, "is the only North in the state of Alabama with a black Infiniti registered in Jefferson County. The address listed is in a Homewood neighborhood, but we drove by the house this morning and no one by the name of North lives there now. The current resident said she didn't know anyone by that name and she's lived in the home with her husband and three kids for five years."

"I take it Mr. North has no record." Of course he didn't. Jess didn't know why she bothered to ask. If he'd had one, the details would already be on that board.

"No criminal record," Lori confirmed. "No prints on file. I ran his name and the MO he used through the usual databases and got nothing. I passed his name along to Agent Manning and he came up empty handed as well. He said he'd run it by his Interpol contact."

Todd Manning was assigned to the Bureau's Birmingham Field Office. He and Jess had worked together a few times. They'd gotten off to a shaky start, but Manning had turned out to be a reliable team player.

"Has anyone driven by the Argyle Drive house today?" Jess had spoken to Gant just before lunch. They'd found nothing new at the house. No evidence that Spears was ever there, not even a fingerprint, and no escape route. It made no sense. He had been there. Four of his hostages had been there. How the hell had he gotten away? How could he not have left a single print? The decision had been made to dismantle the house with the hope of finding evidence. Spears had purchased the property in cash using an alias and a local sleazy attorney who couldn't even describe the purchaser. Which actually made what the Task Force wanted to do much simpler. The transaction had all the earmarks of illegal activity.

"I stopped by," Hayes said. "I spoke to Roark. He said a crew was coming in to start taking down walls. He also mentioned he's moving over to the Gang Task Force to replace Captain Allen." Hayes flashed a fake smile. "In case anyone cares."

No surprise there. Roark was Black's right-hand man. Jess had expected he would be moving up the food chain. Captain Allen remained missing, presumed dead, it was time to fill the position and an opportunity for Black to give Roark a promotion.

Allen was another dark cloud hanging over Dan. Jess had butted heads with Ted Allen early on in her new career with the BPD. To Allen's way of thinking, she had stepped on his toes or unsettled his deal with the very gang element he was sworn to bring to justice. He was suspected of having planted a bomb in her department issued vehicle and of tampering with her personal vehicle. Then he'd promptly disappeared. No one had seen or heard from him in more than a month. He left a wife and family as well as a long, distinguished career with the department. His cell phone and wedding band had both turned up at Dan's former home, suggesting he had something to do with Allen's disappearance. The friction between Jess and Allen had lent credence to the ridiculous theory.

Anyone with half a brain should recognize a setup as blatant as that one. The only questions in Jess's mind was how much of the set up was Spears, and if it wasn't him, then who? Could the mayor really want Dan out that badly? Ridiculous question. Jess was nearly certain Mayor Joseph Pratt had somehow forced Meredith Dority to make allegations of misconduct against Dan going back to his time as liaison between the mayor's office and the department. With Dority dead, they might never know the truth.

"Anything new on the Dority case?" Jess surveyed her team. They weren't working that case, but cops had their own grapevine.

Meredith Dority had been murdered in her mother's home. The neighborhood was one primarily occupied by retired folks. Yet, no one questioned thus far had noticed a single thing. Mrs. Dority was bedridden, recovering from surgery, and unfortunately, she was the reason Dan was a person of interest in the case. She'd heard the argument between Dan and her daughter that morning. She'd even heard the door slam as Dan left. The trouble was that someone else had come into the house almost immediately after Dan left. The mother hadn't been able to hear the discussion between her daughter and the second visitor well enough to identify the voice or to exclude Dan. She could only confirm that the visitor was male and that there was a struggle.

A very bad break for Dan.

Harper shook his head. "The new assistant coroner says it was manual strangulation. Judging by the bruise pattern she agrees that the attacker was male and damned strong. The vic's hyoid bone was broken."

"We have a new assistant coroner?" Jess didn't remember Sylvia mentioning anyone new coming on board.

"Toni James," Lori supplied. "Young, pretty, and bossy."

"Really?" Hayes inquired. "How pretty?"

Lori rolled her eyes. She looked particularly nice today. The well-fitted slacks and feminine pullover were her usual fare, but there was a glow about her. Jess decided that being engaged to the man she loved agreed with her. So much had changed for Lori and her over the past few weeks. One of their first personal conversations had been about how their careers were their top priorities. Jess couldn't help smiling. Now they were both planning weddings and Jess was pregnant.

She had barely managed to get the red skirt she loved so much to zip this morning. The belted jacket was her favorite. She might as well get used to the idea that she'd have to stick with the looser, stretchier outfits she'd finally taken the time to purchase. Oh well, gaining weight was a necessary part of the process. She abruptly realized that Cook was the only member of her team who didn't know about the baby. She'd have to share that news with him on her next visit to the hospital.

"My grandmother had a saying," Lori explained to Hayes, "pretty is as pretty does. We'll just see how Dr. James holds up when we have a couple of victims with their hearts ripped out of their chests."

Hayes looked to Harper and the sergeant shook his head in answer to the question about the new assistant coroner's level of prettiness. "I got nothing, man."

Jess laughed. It was nice to have even a glimmer of relief from the tension.

"On a more professional note," Lori said pointedly, "I ran into a friend at lunch who passed along some good news. She works on the Gang Task Force with Valerie Prescott. Apparently, Prescott withdrew her EEO complaint against Chief Burnett. Prescott claimed it wasn't worth the trouble and she was putting the past behind her."

"That is good news," Jess agreed. Lieutenant Prescott had been most unhappy when Jess was chosen for the position of deputy chief of SPU. Not being selected to take Allen's position added insult to injury and, apparently, prompted Prescott to file the complaint against Dan.

"The EEOC would have seen through her allegations anyway," Harper added.

Jess wished the rest of the false claims against Dan would go away so easily.

Silence lapsed for a few moments. The topic they needed to address now was immensely personal to Jess. As much as she wanted to know the truth about her father, she wasn't looking forward to what she might find out about him. It was bad enough he'd cheated on his wife. If he had been a murderer to boot…She couldn't wrap her mind around the inconceivable theory.

"Moving on." Jess folded her arms over her chest. It was Saturday. Her team had worked back-to-back murder cases for weeks now. No one wanted to waste precious time. "Where are we on the reverend's notes and my mother's journal?"

Lori and Harper exchanged a look. The relationship between Jess and these two went well beyond the professional. Jess considered Lori a close friend. Harper, too, really. It was the first time in her career she'd had personal relationships with her co-workers, whatever their rank. There was a special bond between them and Jess valued it greatly.

Harper turned the case board around. The board stood on wheeled legs, which allowed their ongoing work to be hidden by simply turning it around. Since the SPU office consisted of only one large room there was no privacy for interviewing family members or potential expert witnesses. The moveable case board made discretion possible.

As Jess surveyed the timeline her detectives had built, she was stunned. When had they found the time to do all this?

"We worked on this most of the night." Lori gestured to the timeline. "We believe, based on your mother's journal, that the trouble began when you were approximately three years old. The journal entries before that time are more carefree and routine."

Jess braced her hands on the desk on either side of her. From the day a photo of her father had been discovered at the Brownfield's *body farm*, she and her sister Lily had started to question all that they remembered about their shared childhood. Accusations made by Amanda Brownfield that their father had been some sort of murderer had haunted Jess's dreams for two weeks. The problem was she couldn't trust anything Amanda said. Though some truth was sprinkled amid the lies, there was no way to be certain what was truth and what was fiction.

Then Reverend Gordon Henshaw had been murdered just six days ago. Since then they had discovered the reverend had started his own abrupt and frantic search for the truth surrounding the deaths of Jess's parents. His confusing notes and the pages of her mother's journal painted a startling picture of the final years of Lee and Helen Harris's lives. Although Lori had made Jess a copy of the pages, she hadn't been able to bring herself to read them just yet. She'd had far too many other things going on. Then again, maybe that was nothing but an excuse.

Did she really want to know the whole truth?

"Using the system I developed for lifting hidden messages from the reverend's notes," Harper began, "we believe that your father was lured into some sort of service. Possibly for the United States government."

Hayes got up from his desk and moved closer to the board. He surveyed the copies of the pages they'd found in the reverend's rented hotel room. The reverend had basically disappeared two months ago when he started dissecting the journal. He'd hidden himself in a downtown hotel room. Jess had few memories of the man who had served as the minister in the small Irondale church her family had attended eons ago. She deeply regretted the fear and suffering he had no doubt experienced at the hands of one of Spears's followers.

"Have you queried the various Alabama law enforcement agencies?" Hayes looked to Lori and then to Harper.

"We didn't want to take that step without discussing it with you first," Harper explained before sending a questioning look at Jess.

The lieutenant turned to her. "I'd like to look into that aspect of the investigation, with your permission, of course."

The look that passed between Lori and Harper was easy to read. They were not happy that Hayes

DEBRA WEBB

was horning in on their territory. So maybe things weren't going any more smoothly.

"Please do, Lieutenant," Jess encouraged. She glanced at Lori, and then Harper. "We're a team. I'm sure we'd all appreciate your efforts."

Properly chastised, Lori turned her attention back to the timeline they had created. "Something happened in Jackson County when you were approximately five years old. That's when your father started spending time there, but we haven't been able to nail down any sort of case that might have been conducted at state or federal level. Whatever Lee Harris was working on, it was either personal or top secret, whether legal or not."

"You're saying his involvement with the Brownfield family was limited to a shorter period of time than we thought?" Jess wasn't sure how Lori could be making that conclusion.

"One passage refers to the *summer their innocence died*," Harper pointed to one of the pages. "We believe that's the timeframe Lee was tasked to become involved with the Brownfields. We can't say at what point he became intimately involved with Amanda's mother, but we think it happened that summer. His involvement on some level may have continued from that point until his death."

"Wait." Jess tried to recall Amanda's birthday. "Amanda was born in March the year I turned four."

"March twenty-ninth," Lori confirmed.

Jess nodded. "The timeline is correct." They just had no idea if her father's involvement with the family started long before Amanda was conceived or if the affair was sudden and short. It remained unclear if his connection to the family or to the case was long term or on again off again.

Harper directed everyone's attention to yet another page on the timeline. "This page tells us Helen," Harper cleared his throat, "your mother often had no idea where he would be or for how long."

Jess frowned. "How would she know about the Brownfields then?"

"Maybe your father told her," Lori suggested. "Wanda Newsom insists that Helen warned her to stay away because of the bad people when you were about seven."

Wanda was Helen's sister. Jess had scarcely seen her aunt since she and Lil were taken from her home just a year after their parents' deaths. Wanda hadn't been able to straighten her life out even to care for her dead sister's children.

"I believe something catastrophic happened with the Brownfield case," Harper said. "Something deeply personal to your family that caused them to have to look over their shoulders for the remainder of their lives."

Jess couldn't hold back her anger. "It's called infidelity, Sergeant. My father screwed around with Margaret Brownfield and got her pregnant." The anger faded instantly and hurt took its place.

Lori looked from the endless pages on the case board to Jess. "You know, I find it strange that your mother would seem so worried about the man who'd cheated on her and fathered a child with another woman. If he brought all this down on them, she had to be angry with him. Those passages must be missing."

Everyone in the room was looking at Jess, waiting for her to respond. "I know I would have been mad as hell." She walked to the board and studied the highlighted lines from the pages. "You make an excellent point, those passages have to be missing."

Jess could just imagine the fear and uncertainty her mother faced on hers and Lily's behalf. With Spears still out there, Jess wrapped her arms around her middle, she was terrified for the child she carried. A mother's need to protect her child was instinctive and fierce. A woman with two daughters would have wanted to protect them above all else, wouldn't she?

"When we find the music box," Harper moved closer to her and pointed to the photo of the key discovered in the dead reverend's mouth, "maybe we'll find some answers."

Jess nodded since emotion had once again stolen her ability to speak. Being pregnant made her more emotional than usual. How was she supposed to maintain any perspective with the investigation into whether or not her parents were murdered?

"The music box is the key," Hayes said, almost to himself.

Managing to hold back the tears and further embarrassment, Jess agreed, "You're both right.

The music box is the key. When we find it, we'll have some answers." Jess stared at the photo of the key that presumably unlocked the music box. "The question is how did Spears come to have possession of it? Assuming he does."

Wanda couldn't remember what happened to the music box. She'd sold most of their parents' belongings to support her bad habits. Jess wanted to hate her for what she'd done, or to continue pretending the woman didn't exist as she'd done for the past twenty years. Somehow, she couldn't do either.

"My money's on the reverend," Lori said. "He knew where the box was and Spears followed him to it."

Jess so looked forward to the opportunity of putting a bullet in that bastard's head. "If it wasn't in the hotel room with the reverend, then where?" The chapel where he'd been murdered had been searched top to bottom. His home had been searched as a secondary crime scene. "We should check the chapel and his home again. The church in Irondale, too. Just to be certain."

"What about your childhood home?" Hayes said.

He and Jess had been there yesterday. "We've searched that place several times already."

"One more time won't hurt," Hayes countered.

"Why not? Harper, you and Detective Wells take the reverend's home and Lieutenant Hayes and I will go back to the Irondale house."

Seemed like a good plan since the Argyle house was swarming with Gant's people. First, though, Jess had a stop to make.

MOTT STREET RESIDENCE. 3:00 P.M.

Maddie Brownfield was immensely happy to see Jess. The little girl's reaction had Jess fighting those damned tears again. They sat on the blanket in the backyard and discussed the new doll Jess had brought her.

"Her hair's like mine." Maddie played with the doll's long blond curls.

"It sure is." Jess grinned. "And she has brown eyes just like you, too."

Maddie reached up and touched Jess's hair and then her cheek next to her eye. "You got 'em, too."

Jess nodded. "That's right." It was time to take a small move toward permanence with Maddie. Lily was taking the steps to adopt her and Jess was thrilled to hear it. She'd considered the same. Dan had agreed to support whatever decision she made. Lily had urged them both to allow her to adopt Maddie. Lily's two kids were off in college now. She and Blake had the house all to themselves, and as a nurse Lily was fully equipped to handle whatever special needs Maddie might have presently or in the future. That was the part that swayed Jess's decision. A psychopathic serial killer had raised Maddie, there was no way to know all the terrible things she'd experienced in her young life. She would need plenty of attention in addition to proper counseling. Lily wanted to take on that challenge. She'd reminded Jess that she and Dan were having their first child, they both had stressful jobs, making her the better candidate to be Maddie's new mom.

"I've been thinking, Maddie." The little girl stared up at Jess with those Harris brown eyes. "I'd like you to call me Aunt Jess. Would you like that?"

Maddie smiled and nodded enthusiastically. "Can I come live with you?"

Jess's heart ached for the child. "How about when I get moved into my new house you come stay with me sometimes? We can sleep in sleeping bags in a tent in the backyard. Wouldn't that be fun?"

Maddie nodded again. "Can 'Manda come?"

Jess stilled. This was the first time Maddie had asked about her mother. The counselor had discussed Amanda's death with Maddie. Had the little girl not understood that her mother was dead?

"Who do you mean?" Jess asked, keeping her tone light.

Maddie held up the doll. "My dollie. She's named af'er my mommy. Mommy's an angel now."

"What a nice way to remember your mom." Jess smiled. "Of course, she can come. We wouldn't want to leave her out."

"Can *Wilwee* come?"

Jess laughed. "Do you mean my sister Lily?"

Maddie nodded again, her eyes sparkling. The child really liked Lily.

"Lily can definitely come. We'll have lots of fun."

Maddie jumped up and danced around the yard, holding her doll in the air as if she were flying. There were so many awful things about her mother that Maddie didn't understand. Was it better to keep those horrors a secret or to eventually tell the little girl? Jess knew quite well what the shrinks and the medical journals would say. Maddie would need to face the past one day.

But not today.

CHAPTER FIVE

Lori Wells grabbed another beer from the fridge for Buddy. Chet had invited him over for pizza and to talk about the off-the-record investigation the three of them were undertaking to get the lowdown on Jess's father.

"To Chief Burnett." Chet held up his bottle of Bud Light.

Buddy accepted a cold bottle from Lori and tapped it against Chet's. "Hear, hear. He did me a hell of a favor."

"I'll bet Black was shocked to see Frank Teller strut in there to represent you." Lori grabbed another slice of meat lover's deep-dish pie.

"Damn straight." Buddy laughed. "By the time Frank got through, the DA was all too ready to drop the bribery charges as well as the tampering with evidence charge. Apparently, Black's evidence was way too weak."

"You still a person of interest in the Amanda Brownfield case?" Chet bit off a hunk of pizza.

Buddy nodded. "I got no problem with that. Hell, I was the last one to see her before she escaped. I gave 'em permission to check my cell phone records. I'm confident they'll find I was nowhere near that hospital when she walked." He reached for the last slice of pizza.

Lori dabbed her lips with a napkin. "We found zip at the reverend's house."

"Maybe you're looking too hard." Buddy took a swig of beer. "I figured out a long time ago that when you want to hide something, you hide it some place so obvious no one will bother to look. They're too busy searching for some hard to find spot."

Lori had to admit his reasoning made sense. "We'll keep that in mind next time we examine a scene for evidence."

"You spend as much time dealing with the strange and eccentric like I do and you figure out they go about things pretty simply. They bank on the smart folks overlooking the easy."

"You never thought about coming back to the department?" Chet leaned back in his chair and studied Buddy. "Or did you screw over too many people to have a second chance?"

Lori grimaced. She'd wondered when Chet would get around to confronting Buddy about his partner. She'd kind of hoped it wouldn't happen, that maybe Chet had put it behind him. Guess not.

Buddy sat his empty beer bottle on the table. "I like you, Harper, so let's clear the air once and for all."

"Works for me." Chet deposited his empty bottle on the table as well.

"Sergeant Horace Beard was a decent guy and a damned good cop," Buddy began. "But he made a bad mistake when he married LaNita Kirkpatrick. The woman was nothing but a gold digger."

Lori watched Chet's jaw tighten. She hoped Buddy didn't push too far. Beard had been Chet's first partner.

"She'd slept with half the cops in the department. Everybody knew it but Beard. If you tried to talk about her to him he just got angry. So we let it go."

"Whatever she was," Chet argued, "that gave you no right to have an affair with her."

"True enough." Buddy shrugged. "That's why I didn't."

Chet's gaze narrowed. "Horace told me you slept with her."

"Many times," Buddy agreed. "*Before* she married him. Hell, man, why do you think Internal Affairs cleared me?" Buddy held his arms out wide. "Because I was innocent. There aren't many times in my life I can say I was innocent of whatever I was accused of, but that's one of 'em. I drank too much, got rowdy too many times, but I never messed with another man's wife. Not all the guys on the force felt that way."

Fury painted a path up Chet's neck and across his face. "Who was it then?"

"The same detective who planted that evidence in Horace's home to get him out of the way. The dumbass didn't have sense enough to know that as soon as LaNita got her hands on a little money, she was gone. Sure enough, when Horace died, LaNita took the insurance money and split. She used him the way she used anyone who gave her half a chance."

"I want his name."

Buddy braced his hands on the table. "I tell you what, as soon as Burnett's troubles are cleared up I'll give you his name. But remember, you can't bring Horace back by doing something stupid and screwing up your own career."

"So the guy who did this to Chet's partner is your source," Lori concluded. "The guy was dirty all those years ago and he's still dirty."

Buddy nodded. "The difference is this time he's going down." Buddy stood. "I appreciate the pizza and beer, but I'm gone. I got places to go and people to see." He thrust his hand across the table toward Chet. "We good?"

Chet stared at him for a long moment before he stood and then accepted the offered hand. "We're good."

Lori managed a deep breath for the first time since Chet brought up the subject of his first partner. "You're nudging your contacts about Lee Harris?"

Buddy turned to her. "I've got a guy I'm hoping can find Harris's name in one top secret database or the other. We'll see what he comes up with."

"We appreciate the help." Lee Harris had been in some form of law enforcement. Lori was sure of it.

"This guy," Chet said as he followed Buddy to the door, "is he in the FBI?"

Buddy shook his head. "Retired NSA. He still has connections. If he can't find Harris then he was the kind of employee they don't keep files on."

The idea made Lori shudder. She had a feeling they had only scratched the surface when it came to Jess's father.

When Buddy was gone, Lori locked the door behind. When she turned around, Chet trapped her against the door, one muscled arm on either side of her.

He leaned in close. "You know what tonight is, don't you?"

Lori grinned. "Saturday night."

He nodded. "We haven't had sex in two nights because of work."

"We could have this morning except Chester called." Lori licked her lips. Chet's gaze followed the move. "As much as I love sex with you, it was good to hear his sweet little voice."

Chester was Chet's three-year-old son. He and his mother had left Birmingham until this Spears business was over. In the beginning Lori hadn't appreciated the way Chet's ex had snuck out of town with their son, but she'd done the right thing. Chester was safe this way.

Chet smiled. "I can't wait until he's home." He leaned closer still and kissed her neck.

Lori shivered. One day she and Chet would be making babies of their own. That, too, would have to wait until this Spears nightmare was over and there was time for Chet to have his vasectomy reversed. She could wait. Right now, just knowing how much Chet loved her and that she was going to be his wife was enough.

She reached for the buttons of his shirt. "We haven't had sex in the shower for ages." They usually ended up in the big, jetted tub in the master bathroom.

"The shower it is." He shrugged out of his shirt and lifted her into his arms.

Lori wrapped her legs around his waist as she peeled off her blouse. While he carried her to the bathroom she removed her bra. She was so wet she could hardly stand to wait another second.

Chet reached into the shower and turned on the faucet. Lori allowed her legs to slide down his body until her feet were on the floor. They tore off the rest of each other's clothes and climbed beneath the hot spray of water. He lifted her against his chest once more. Her legs locked around his waist and she sank down onto him. She screamed with the incredible sensation of being filled by the man she loved with her whole heart.

Whether it was fifteen minutes later or thirty she couldn't say, by the time the water had cooled he'd made her come three times. When he came, she closed her eyes and imagined the time when this incredible act of pleasure would give them a child.

She and Jess would be first time mothers together.

Lori thought of Chad lying in that hospital room and what a miracle it was that he'd survived. She hugged Chet tighter and whispered in his ear. "I love you."

He smiled, his lips tickling her forehead. "I love you."

Spears would not take this man from her.

CHAPTER SIX

Jess sat on the floor snuggled up to the coffee table with Lily. The puppy was curled up under the table. They'd been studying the pages of their mother's journal for the past hour and a half and found nothing that solved the mystery of who Lee Harris was or what he did when he was away from home.

Lil pushed aside her empty bowl. She'd made the most wonderful salad with all sorts of tender greens and delicious fruits. Jess couldn't remember the last time she'd enjoyed a meatless salad more. The puppy had munched on croutons. Lil had prepared an extra salad for Dan and tucked it in the fridge. Jess wasn't sure what time he would be home. Since he couldn't be a part of the official investigation, he was helping with the boots-on-the-ground search for Nina like hundreds of other private citizens.

Calling Dan a private citizen felt wrong. He'd been a cop and a public servant for far too many years. He didn't deserve this humiliating treatment.

74

"These entries go right along with what I remember about life before Mom and Dad died."

Jess flipped through the plastic encased pages. "You're right." She read a few entries. "The pages read exactly the way I remember things. There isn't a single entry that explains anything really. All the trouble is woven into Reverend Henshaw's notes, and none of it makes sense."

"Like a puzzle or a riddle."

Jess nodded. "If we discount the possibility that the reverend may have gone off the deep end, that leaves us with the scenario that as a man of God bound by rules of privilege, he was Mom's only outlet. She couldn't tell anyone else her fears. All she could do was keep friends and Wanda away as the situation became worse."

Lil seemed to consider Jess's words for a moment. "I don't remember Mom having any friends. Dad was never home enough to have friends over. Work kept him away, or at least that's what she always said." Lil laughed, the sound derisive. "I don't remember any holiday dinners or barbecues with friends gathered around like the photo you found."

"Neither do I." Jess stared at the pages again. "What I remember is right here. In the journal pages." Jess bit her lips together, hesitated to say what she was thinking. She had to say it. "Do you think this," she placed her hand on the binder of pages, "is what she wanted us to remember?"

Lil's eyes widened. "The truth was too terrible and she wanted to protect us from it so she only let us see and hear the fairytale she wished was real."

Jess made a face. "A sort of well-meaning brainwashing?"

Lil nodded. "They never let us hear their private conversations about the fear or the worries related to whatever was going on. It was a way of protecting us, I guess."

"She warned Wanda off so she wouldn't ask questions or stumble onto anything that might have her demanding answers." Or, that would get her killed, Jess didn't mention.

Lil hugged herself. "How awful that must have been for Mom."

"Stuck at the house alone with us for days and weeks while he was God knows where." Anger stirred in Jess. "What kind of husband and father does that to his family? Where was Mom's outrage? Her husband cheated on her. Fathered a child with another woman! Whatever he was involved in took both of them away from us."

Lil made a pained face. "Let's give him the benefit of the doubt until we know the whole story."

"If," Jess reminded her, "we ever do."

"He was always good to us, Jess. Mom never tried to take us and leave. She never spoke badly about him. Those things have to mean something."

"Where would she go? To live with Wanda?" Jess shook her head. "Fear is a powerful motivator, Lil. Maybe he wanted her scared so she wouldn't leave him. From what I know, so far, he was involved with Margaret—with that family—for more than a one-night stand. If he really loved us, I can't believe he wouldn't have found a way out."

"He loved us. I know he did. He was trapped somehow. That's the only possible explanation."

"Maybe you're right." Jess closed the binder. Despite the bits and pieces she had learned in Scottsboro, she had no ironclad evidence of anything other than two undeniable facts—their father was somehow involved with the Brownfields and he'd had a child with Margaret. "Lieutenant Hayes and I went back to the Irondale house this afternoon, but we found nothing. No secret hiding place where the music box might be stashed. Not one thing that prompted any memories."

"Do you think Spears has the music box?"

"Yes. I do." To Jess, it was the only scenario that made any sense. "Otherwise, why would he have the key?"

"Do you believe he was really in that house on Argyle Drive?" Lil chafed her arms as if she felt a chill. "That's not so far from here, you know."

"He was there. Buddy saw him." Lil was right. It was too damned close. "We caught him off guard." Jess smiled. "I can just imagine how furious he is at the idea that one of his trusted followers dared to defy him."

"Will he try some kind of payback?" A new worry clouded Lil's face. "Does that put you or Dan in greater danger?"

Jess considered how best to answer her question. Nothing she said would be particularly reassuring. "It puts a kink in his plan, that's for sure.

Spears is a sociopath with a grandiose sense of self-worth. For one, he's a perfectionist. He's controlling and obsessive." She shook her head. "Not to mention an extreme narcissist. He believes he's too brilliant to be caught. He doesn't take responsibility for anything. Someone else is always responsible when things go wrong. This failure could set off a chain reaction of erratic behavior or it could make him more determined to ensure there are no more mistakes—no matter the cost. Unfortunately, it's impossible to predict how he'll react."

"But you almost caught him once before," Lil reminded her. "How did he react that time?"

"What happened before was one of his games. He set me up to find him. This time is different." Whatever came next Jess fully understood that it would be over the top. Spears would need to prove his superiority. Her sister was correct, vengeance would be a priority.

The warning that someone was on the stairs outside had Jess popping up to check the security monitor. The puppy raced to the door in that unco-ordinated lope of his. Jess smiled. "It's Dan."

"And my cue to go home." Lil got up and grabbed her purse. "Blake won't be home until around midnight." She draped her purse straps on her shoulder. "But that's okay because I have my nice young officer to escort me home and watch out for me."

Jess gave her a hug. "I'm hoping this will be over soon."

Lil nodded. "You'll get him and then we can all sleep at night."

"Text me when you get home," Jess ordered.

"I will. Promise."

Lil and Dan exchanged hugs at the door. He tried to convince her to stay a while longer, but she begged off. Lil could see how tired he was as well as Jess could. This whole situation was taking a heavy toll on him. No matter that he and Meredith had been divorced for sixteen or so years, he had still considered her a friend. He scarcely had time to grieve for her with Spears playing his games and with Nina missing.

The puppy dancing around them, Jess hugged Dan hard and then she searched his face. "Still nothing?"

He shook his head. "It's like she vanished into thin air. Nothing on the security cameras at the center where she lived. None of the residents or personnel saw or heard a single thing. Not one valid report of a sighting from the public despite the huge reward the Senator is offering."

"I keep hoping the clinic somehow fell down on the job and that Nina is just out there wandering around lost. The alternative is unthinkable." Jess shuddered. The idea that Nina could be with Spears was even more disturbing given her mental illness. The longer she was off the meds she needed, the more unstable she would become. Wherever she was, Nina was going through hell.

Jess closed the door and locked it. "I saw Gina's special about Nina on the news. She did a really great job. I can't imagine anyone seeing her story and not being moved to act."

"Let's hope so."

Gina Coleman was Birmingham's award-winning television investigative reporter. She was the best at putting heart into a story and at conveying it in a way that tugged on the emotions. It didn't hurt that she was gorgeous as well as respected and immensely popular. She was a good friend. To Jess and to Dan.

"Lil made you a salad. Sit and I'll do the serving." Jess glanced back at him as she padded to the fridge. "Fair warning there's no meat, but it's scrumptious." Never in her life had food tasted so good. Lil had warned that changes in taste and cravings were part of being pregnant. So far Jess's favorite snack was still M&Ms, but everything she put in her mouth tasted better lately.

Dan pulled out a chair at the table and had a seat. The puppy hadn't stopped vying for his attention since he walked in so Dan scratched him behind the ears. It was strange having him come home dressed in jeans and a casual shirt rather than his usual elegant suits. Even on Saturdays, if he went to work, he dressed the part of chief of police. Not today. *So not fair.*

"Gina wants to do an in-depth feature story on my life to go with an exclusive on my career when I'm reinstated." He made a sound that was far too dry to be called a laugh. "I warned her that might be a little premature."

Jess placed the salad and dressing and a cold beer in front of him. "You listen to me, Daniel Thomas Burnett, you will be cleared and reinstated. Soon." She placed a fork and napkin next to his bowl. "Gina's smart to get the ball rolling on a feature story. Birmingham loves you. When this is over, they're going to want the whole story. And then they'll love you more."

He leaned over and left a soft kiss on her cheek. "I love you."

Jess smoothed a hand over his beard-stubbled jaw. "I love you more. Now eat. We have houses to look at."

"We do?" He added dressing to his salad and dug in.

"Your mother's realtor friend, Nancy Wolfe, emailed me several potential homes." Jess hadn't mentioned realtors to Lily. The last time a friend of Lil's had been lured into showing Jess a house she'd ended up a victim of Spears's protégé, Matthew Reed. Besides, Lil would insist on showing Jess only houses close to her. Though Jess loved her sister she didn't want to live next door to her any more than she wanted to live too close to Dan's parents.

"Great." He stabbed a tomato with his fork. "Did you see one you liked?"

"Three actually," Jess admitted. She'd gone into this house hunting business with serious reluctance only to discover that looking was addictive. The more houses she toured the more she wanted to see. "All in our preferred neighborhood."

Dan set his fork aside. "*Our* preferred neighborhood?"

That was another thing Jess had realized. "I kind of like Mountain Brook. Once you realize most of the Brookies are just regular people, it's not so bad."

A grin spread across his handsome face. "So we're not all snobs?"

She stole a cucumber. "Not all."

"Why don't you bring the laptop over here and we'll have a look at these three houses you like so much."

Jess scooted back her chair and went for the laptop. "Lil and Blake hired an attorney to begin the adoption process."

"That's great. They'll be terrific parents for Maddie."

Jess readied the laptop and resumed her seat. "They will. She said the kids are excited about having a little sister."

Blake Junior and Alice were off at college, and Lil was not adapting to the empty nest situation very well. It was the perfect solution. After all, Maddie was their niece. She belonged in the family. It was impossible to think of Maddie without thinking of Amanda. Jess had already asked Lori to secure some of the family photos taken from the Brownfield farm so they could be saved for Maddie.

"So here we go." Jess clicked on the details section of the first house. "This one is nice. I think my favorite part is the nursery."

Two of the houses were brick with Georgian style architecture and one was a Tudor with a rock facade. They were all quite stately, but not pretentious. Big yards and easy commutes into the city.

"We might have to paint the nursery blue," Dan teased.

"And we might not," Jess countered. The room was a soft shade of pink with pastel green accents. Little girls should have pink rooms, so said Lily anyway.

When a photo of the patio with its outdoor kitchen appeared on the screen, Dan let loose with a long low whistle. "Now that's what I call a grill station."

Jess had no idea why men appeared to love going outside in ninety-five degree heat to stand over a blazing grill. It was far too easy to go to Logan's or Outback where the steaks were grilled in an air-conditioned kitchen. "There's a screened porch, too." That was her favorite outdoor space. Mosquitos were a nuisance in the south.

They moved through the photos of the other two houses, discussing pros and cons about each. By the time they were finished, they had moved to the sofa.

"We should tour these three," Dan suggested.

"I'll work in the appointments as soon as possible." The realtor had given Jess a warning about how swiftly properties moved in the Mountain Brook area. They needed to act quickly. This baby was coming in April. Buying a house, making it their own, and settling in was a big job. She absolutely did not want to be nearing her due date, working, and trying to move all at the same time. She'd heeded the many warnings from her sister as well as from the books she'd been reading.

"Why don't we shoot for tomorrow?" Dan closed the laptop. "If you're free."

Though it would be Sunday, realtors worked seven days a week—so said Ms. Wolfe anyway. Jess and her team were still attempting to piece together the evidence the reverend had left behind, but she could spare a few hours. "I'll send the realtor a text and see how her schedule looks."

"We could have a nice lunch and enjoy a rare day off." He traced her cheek with the tip of his finger. "In a few months we won't be just a couple anymore. We'll be a family with another person's wants and needs to consider."

Jess's heart beat a little faster at the idea. She'd decided ages ago there wouldn't be any children for her. Her one brief marriage hadn't worked out. She and her ex had ended up where they'd started—as friends. Dan had been a world away with three short marriages behind him. Jess had adjusted to the idea that she would be happy as a career woman and she'd prepared for that path. Then she'd come back here and everything had changed. They had both realized that their marriages had failed because they had never stopped loving each other—not in twenty years.

She smiled. She was so glad she'd come home. Her arms went around his neck. "I was thinking that we could take the puppy for a stroll and then we could close him up in the bathroom for a little privacy. If we turn the music loud enough he might not bark at all." Wishful thinking.

"How about we take the puppy for a walk and then we go for a ride? I know a couple of really cool make-out spots we frequented back in the day."

Memories of all the places they'd made love as crazy teenagers had her feeling giddy. "I like your plan much better."

"I'll get the leash."

Jess grabbed her shoes and watched as Dan prepared the puppy for a walk. He was going to be a great father.

CHAPTER SEVEN

Eric Spears paced back and forth. The dingy warehouse was beneath him. Far beneath him. This was completely unacceptable.

A single bare bulb glowed overhead. His tools were reduced to several rudimentary knives and a handgun lying atop a dirty wooden table. He needed *his* tools. Each perfectly weighted one had been a precision instrument. Now look at him! He clenched and unclenched his fists as he paced. How was he supposed to finish the game without his tools...without the guests he had so painstakingly selected?

He couldn't finish the game...everything was ruined.

He had to think. If there was time, he could retrieve the necessary assets, reorganize, and acquire an appropriate place in which to conduct his game. *If* he had more time he could replace the tools so essential to his needs...but he didn't have time.

"There is no time!" His voice echoed in the vast empty space.

A whimper drew him to a halt. He turned slowly and stared at the woman clumsily tied to a chair. Fear rose in her, making her shudder and sob until mucus ran from her nose, joining the stream of hot, salty tears on her face.

How immensely pathetic. He moved toward her and peered down into those rich brown eyes. They were swollen from the many, many hopeless tears she had shed. The gag stuffed into her mouth forced her lush lips to bulge with the tiniest scrap of the dingy cloth protruding between them.

His gaze drifted down to her bare breasts. The perfect mounds rose and fell with the sobs quaking through her. Sheer terror had her nipples standing erect. Thick, firm nipples adorned her heavy breasts. Rare was the woman born with such high perfect breasts. Her narrow waist flared into hips that curved gently, guiding an admirer's greedy gaze down the long length of well-toned legs.

As beautiful as she was with that long mane of dark, silky hair, she was still an utterly tragic creature useful for nothing more than giving him pleasure.

"Soon," he whispered. "I will touch you in ways no other man has dared. Your last thought will be of me as you draw your final frantic breath. Then you'll die, cold and alone like all the others."

She looked away and sobbed even harder.

He laughed. "What was God thinking when he created such wretched creatures?"

Turning his back, he focused on the other matter requiring his attention. Eric shook his head.

"Quentin, you have disappointed me so." He sighed. "I had such high hopes for you."

Quentin North stared at the floor, trying to pretend he hadn't been looking at the woman—the naked, terrified woman tied with her legs spread wide apart, revealing her vulgar secrets. He sat on a stool far too short for his height, his long arms folded over his lap to hide a bulging erection. He appeared awkward, like a rutting teenage boy who only wanted to stick his dick in something but couldn't quite work up the nerve.

"What do you have to say for yourself?" Eric demanded.

"I've done everything you asked." Feeling humble or merely terrified, Quentin kept his gaze lowered as he spoke. "My only failure was in trusting Amanda too much. She tricked me."

"Tricked you?" Eric laughed, the sound echoing off the dusty, decrepit walls. "You permitted that useless bitch to see things she should not have seen." Had Eric known he would have played just a little longer before ending her infinitely pointless life. "Look what it has cost me!" He spread his arms wide to indicate the shabby accommodations.

Quentin said nothing.

Frustration roared through Eric. "It takes time to recover from a breach such as this and I do not have the luxury of time." He closed his eyes and shook his head. "Your ineptness has ruined everything. How can I achieve the grand finale I desire when you have crippled my efforts so?"

Quentin lifted his gaze, evidently feeling a miniscule burst of defiance. "Why not ask for help from your many dedicated followers?"

Eric swiped the knife from the table and had the blade against the fool's throat before the thought to recoil formed in his woefully inadequate brain. "You know very well why I cannot ask anyone for help."

Quentin had the audacity to smile. "You've killed all those who stepped forward to serve you. Now the rest have abandoned you. You have no one left except me. You *need* me."

Eric nicked his throat. Blood bloomed then slid beneath the collar of his cheap shirt. "Do you really believe that such a dire circumstance—if it were true—would be your salvation? Tsk, Tsk, Quentin, you truly are a fool."

"I don't see anyone else? Who's going to carry out the tasks you require?"

Now he was simply begging for his life. "Any moron could accomplish such meager tasks, Quentin."

"I've done more for you than all the others. I killed five people and still found time to watch Burnett for the perfect moment to destroy him. The police believe he killed his ex-wife. Outside of a miracle, his life is over. Just think what they'll do to him in prison."

Eric wasn't so convinced, though the mere concept ignited a fire in his loins. "That should have been the case with the cop who despised Jess so, but that endeavor hasn't fared so well has it?"

"I told you I was preempted on that one. Someone else took Allen out. It wasn't my mistake. How could I finish the task when he vanished?"

"Perhaps you're right." Eric was quite certain Dan Burnett possessed neither the stomach nor the balls for such a move. "I suppose some of his drug dealing friends had a score to settle."

"Sounds right to me."

Eric traced the vee of Quentin's shirt with the tip of the knife. "Do you think for one second that I care what sounds right to you?" He ripped into the flesh there.

Quentin flinched but didn't make a sound as more blood trickled down his chest. "I took pictures for you tonight."

Eric had ordered him to watch Jess closely. He needed to know her every move if there was to be any chance of salvaging some reasonable climax to his game. When it was done, he intended to take a long vacation far from this place. Far from the memories of her.

"Pictures you say?"

Quentin reached into his shirt pocket and removed a slim stack of photos. "I think you'll like these."

Eric flipped through the photos, devouring each one. He caressed the image of Jess, blood smearing across the glossy surface. She sat astraddle Burnett, her head thrown back and her breasts jutting forward. Eric's body grew harder as the images played out in his mind's eye. Burnett disappeared and Eric took his place, lying there as Jess rode him with that same look of ecstasy on her face. Then he would roll her over and pound into her. All the while his fingers would be tightening around her delicate throat. He would squeeze until the final breath sputtered from those lush lips and he came hard inside her. He always wore a condom, but with Jess he wouldn't. He wanted his seed to rain against her uterus as Dan's child withered and died inside her lifeless body.

"Where?" he demanded, scarcely able to speak.

"I followed them to Sloss Furnaces. I thought you would like to see."

Eric calmed his breathing and tucked the photos into his trouser pocket before settling his attention back on the albatross in front of him. "You were correct, Quentin."

"Does that make up for my mistake?"

Eric laughed long and loud. "Did you really believe your inept attempts to distract me would save you?"

"I believe," Quentin dared to glower at him, "you're losing it, that's what I believe."

Eric buried the knife in his chest, wiggling the blade just so to ensure it slid deep between his ribs and into his heart. Blood gushed around his fingers, the warmth making him hard all over again.

"Do you know what I did to the last man who said those words to me, Quentin?" Eric watched as the life disappeared from his eyes. "I chopped him into very small pieces." The memory of warm blood spurting against his flesh took Eric's breath. His heart pounded with enough force to fracture his sternum.

Before he could restrain the urge, he strode across the room and stared at the glass case hanging on the wall. He smiled, pleasure now coursing like liquid fire through his veins. "That will do quite nicely." He removed the one useful object in the abysmal place and returned to Quentin's miserable corpse.

"Where to begin?" Eric assessed the situation a moment, tightened his grip on the heavy wood handle and then lifted the fire ax high above his head. He slammed the ax into Quentin's shoulder, absorbing the impact of muscle and bone.

The stupid bitch behind him tried to scream and gagged.

Eric turned to her and smiled as the blood dripped, still warm, down his arms. "Don't worry, you'll have your turn."

CHAPTER EIGHT

They had stopped by the hospital to see Chad Cook who was doing much better. Jess noted visible improvement and that made her happy. Cook's parents were impressed that Chief of Police Dan Burnett had visited their son. If they'd even heard about Dan's current status they didn't seem to care. Jess had opted to wait on sharing the news about the baby since Cook's parents had been visiting. There was plenty of time.

Senator Robert Baron had called and asked to see Jess, cutting their visit with Cook short. Jess had been immensely grateful she'd chosen her new sapphire dress and matching summer cardigan this morning. A command performance at the senator's home hadn't been on her agenda. Thankfully, she was dressed for the occasion. Senator Baron was a nice man, but a request from him, personal or not, still carried the influence of his office.

Dan had driven her to the Baron estate. He was now having coffee and discussing the expanding search for Nina with Sylvia and her mother on the back terrace. Jess had declined refreshments since her breakfast of toast and yogurt wasn't sitting so well. She hoped the morning sickness wasn't gathering a second wind. Senator Baron had invited her to his study. She'd settled into one of the large leather wingback chairs stationed in front of his desk. He stood near the window that provided an extraordinary view of the gardens that adorned the grounds all the way around his grand home.

"I hope you don't mind that I asked to speak with you privately."

Robert Baron was far closer to seventy than to sixty, yet he was as tall and fit as a man half his age. His hair had grayed into that distinguished color that never looked old. He sounded as strong and vibrant as he looked. His bearing spoke of wealth and power, while his personality proved warm and approachable. Jess liked him.

"I don't mind at all, Senator. What would you like to talk about?" She suspected the invitation was about Nina...and Spears.

"My daughter has been missing for seventy-two hours. You're aware the circumstances grow more dire with every passing hour."

Jess understood perfectly. Outside a controlled environment and without her required medication, Nina's condition would deteriorate rapidly, leaving her vulnerable and desperate. "The BPD is doing everything possible to find Nina." Every PI and reporter in the county was chasing the million-dollar reward Baron had announced on Friday afternoon.

"And still," he sighed, "it isn't enough."

Jess wished there were words of encouragement she could share, but the truth was there were none. If Nina Baron was still alive she'd either hidden herself somewhere and was lost or Spears had taken her. Any other kidnapper would be asking for ransom.

Baron rounded the desk and claimed the seat next to Jess. "If this serial killer has my daughter, what are the odds of her survival?"

Forty-eight hours ago Jess would have told him zero. Finding those three women alive had changed everything. "I honestly can't say." Jess considered her words carefully. She did not want to give the man false hope. "I will tell you that if Nina is with Spears her survival will depend solely on how he intends to use her in his game. He's not choosing his victims for his own personal pleasure any more. He's broken that long-term pattern. His actions appear to be about making a particular statement or getting to me—maybe both. We have to be prepared for anything. Particularly now that he's lost his advantage."

A glint of anticipation sparked to life in the Senator's eyes. "You're telling me there's hope my daughter's still alive."

Again, Jess picked her words with great care. "I'm telling you that if Nina is with Spears she will stay alive as long as he needs her and when he doesn't anymore we'll find her body." That was as blunt as she cared to be.

Baron gave a succinct nod. "That's all I wanted to know. Chief Black has been most optimistic, but I felt as if he was telling me what I wanted to hear rather than the hard facts. I appreciate your candor, Jess."

The urge to give him something more to hang onto would not be dismissed. "He has a plan, Senator, we just don't know what it is yet. We do know that it includes me. You have my word, if given the chance, I'll do all I can to protect Nina."

"I don't know you very well, Jess, but somehow I believe you will."

Jess smiled. "I'll take that as a compliment, sir."

He stood. "We should join the others on the terrace. We have another half hour before today's search efforts begin."

Even a search for the missing took a break on Sunday morning for folks to attend church. Nina Baron needed all the help she could get, including prayer.

Senator Baron wrapped Jess's arm around his and escorted her to the terrace. Sylvia and her mother went through the expected etiquette steps, but Jess saw the fear and exhaustion behind their masks.

Hope was waning.

Jess's cell sounded off. Dan winced, understanding what the call likely meant. Jess excused herself and checked the screen.

Lori calling.

"Hey, Lori. What's going on?" Jess held her breath, hoping against hope that neither Nina nor Campbell's body had been discovered.

"We found Quentin North."

Jess glanced over at Dan. "What's the location?"

"He's in his car at Sloss Furnaces."

The location hit Jess like a dash of cold water in the face. "Is there a note or…anything?"

"No note. Just photos of you and…Chief Burnett."

Jess reminded herself to breathe. "I'll be there in half an hour."

Her gaze sought and found Dan's. The two of them had taken a drive to the old Sloss Furnaces last night. Back in high school, the former site where iron had been produced was one of their favorite secret places. Sloss Furnaces was a historic landmark. For nearly a century the old blast furnaces had stood as a reminder of how Birmingham had risen from nothing so quickly, earning it the nickname the Magic City. Over the decades dozens of men had died in the furnaces, including Jess's maternal grandfather. According to some it was one of the most haunted places on earth. Lots of young folks had used the old open-air museum for a secret escape over the years.

Last night she and Dan had made love there…

1ST AVENUE AT 33RD STREET, SLOSS
FURNACES, BIRMINGHAM, 11:55 A.M.

The black Infiniti sedan that had appeared in Jess's life far too frequently in the past few weeks sat in the parking area beneath First Avenue surrounded by crime scene tape. The air was still and thick. The drone of traffic overhead on First Avenue was as steady as the beating of Jess's heart. Two BPD cruisers blocked the area, the uniformed officers keeping the scene secure and searching for a perp or any other victims. The crime scene van arrived at the same time as Jess and Dan. Lori had them standing by while Jess had a look.

Quentin North—or what appeared to be all of him—sat behind the steering wheel in his black Infiniti. His arms and legs were stacked atop his torso in the seat. On top of the neatly arranged pile of body parts was his head. His sunglasses had been tucked into place. Wherever he had died, it hadn't been in this car. Judging by the state of rigor, Jess estimated he'd been here at least seven or eight hours.

Quentin North had been doing Spears's bidding for weeks. Why kill him now? Had he completed his service to Eric Spears? Had Spears drugged him and then killed him or had North sat back and allowed him to have at it? Maybe another follower had taken care of the dirty work. Still, why now? Had North screwed up?

Jess was leaning in that direction. Amanda had described the dark-haired man as the one who'd taken her to Spears. If her seeing that license plate had been unplanned, and clearly it was, North may have been the one to allow it to happen.

Whatever the reason, Spears had used his death to pass along a message to Jess. Photos, printed at a local self-service photo shop, depicted Jess and Dan making love beneath the stars. In each one, Dan had been x'ed out with a red felt-tip marker. Blood, probably North's, was smeared on the photos. Anger mounted inside Jess. She would not allow Spears to hurt Dan. He'd suffered far too much already.

Jess took a breath and reminded herself to consider the situation objectively. As embarrassing as the photos were there was no way around permitting the techs to document them. It had to be done. Dammit.

"Have you ever seen anything like this from Spears?"

Jess looked from the victim to Lori and back. "No. This could mean he has a new follower taking care of business for him."

Or, it could mean that Eric Spears was coming undone.

A clammy feeling seeping under her skin, Jess shook off the idea. Five long years the Bureau had tracked this killer. Dozens of victims had been attributed to his annual killing sprees. None had ever been hacked up like this. He could be trying to throw them off. More likely, he had a new follower leaving his own signature.

"Maybe Spears was pissed," Lori suggested, "about the Amanda thing. Maybe he lost it and went crazy."

"Losing this much power over the situation would be a tremendous blow to his ego." Jess turned away from the gruesome scene. She reached into her bag and fished out her cell to see if she'd missed a message. She couldn't help wondering why Spears hadn't sent her a message about the photos. Why had he suddenly gone silent?

"That new assistant coroner is en route," Harper announced as he tucked his cell back into the holster at his belt.

Jess looked forward to meeting her, but she missed Sylvia. She had come to trust Sylvia's expertise and to count her as a member of their close-knit major crimes team. "You said her name is Toni?"

"Toni James," Harper confirmed.

"Thank you, Sergeant. Let's get a tech over here to document and bag these photos. No point in the new assistant coroner seeing my..." Jess blew out a disgusted breath. "Jesus, I really need to find time to workout."

Lori chuckled. "You look great, Chief."

Jess rolled her eyes. "Right. So, let's see what Mr. North carried in his trunk."

"No dead bodies." Lori walked to the back of the car with Jess. "Lots of spy equipment, ammo, and a mini pharmacy."

"Well, well." Jess surveyed the parabolic listening device, high-powered binoculars, cameras, and lenses. Two Tasers, various ropes, and handcuffs, too. A tote contained hypodermics and a lot of what Jess suspected was Ketamine. "The man was certainly prepared." Jess set her hands on her hips. "A man who travels this prepared wouldn't leave home without his cell phone. Where's his phone?"

"Maybe Spears or whoever killed him took it," Lori suggested as they moved back to the driver's side window to view the pile of naked body parts once more. "I didn't find it in the car and, unless it's in a body cavity, he doesn't have it on him."

"So North took the photos, went and had them processed, and then Spears or one of his followers chopped him up, all within the last twelve or so hours."

"If I could have a look, please," a female voice announced, "I can provide an approximate time of death so you don't have to guess."

Jess and Lori turned to the woman who'd spoken. The new assistant coroner wore practical shoes with no heels whatsoever, khaki slacks, and a blue blouse mostly hidden by a white lab coat. Medium length blond hair framed an attractive face, but there wasn't a smile in sight.

"I'm Deputy Chief Jess Harris," Jess thrust out her hand, "and this is Detective Lori Wells."

"Doctor Toni James." She gave Jess's hand a quick pump. "A pleasure, I'm sure." She acknowledged Lori with a nod.

DEBRA WEBB

Jess decided the lady was from out west somewhere, Colorado maybe. "We'll leave you to it then."
Jess mustered up a smile. "I will, however, need time
of death as soon as possible. My investigation hinges
on that piece of information. The sooner you can
tell me, the sooner we can move forward."

"Then I should get busy."

Jess looked around for Dan. He and Hayes
were helping BPD's finest check out the site.
There were a hell of a lot of places to hide in there
and Dan knew them all. Jess doubted there were
any other victims, but the steps had to be taken.
She and Lori moved toward the entrance of the
industrial site.

"She must be new in town," Lori said with a
glance back at the ME.

"Definitely," Jess agreed, "or she would know I
like time of death first." Why was it ME's insisted on
going through their steps before giving her the one
thing she needed first? It wasn't like the probable
cause of death wasn't glaringly obvious.

"Chief Harris!"

Jess turned back just in time to see the ME stag-
ger back from the open car door. Jess hurried to the
car, somehow managing to keep up with Lori's swift
strides.

"There's something in his mouth," James
advised, "and it's moving."

North's head had fallen over. Jess watched as
something wiggled past the victim's lips and scur-
ried away.

"What the hell?" Lori muttered. "Was that a…?"

"Rat," Jess confirmed. Spears's message was loud and clear. He knew his follower had made the misstep that had ratted him out.

CHAPTER NINE

Eric waited in the car he had acquired for carrying out the ingenious move that had come to him upon waking this morning. He'd taken a room at the finest hotel in Birmingham, and he'd tipped a bellman an enormous sum to do a little shopping for him. The choice in accommodations had been a brilliant strategy. His face was plastered all over local television broadcasts as well as the papers, yet no one expected a cold-blooded serial killer to walk into the only five-star hotel in town. A rental service had delivered a Lexus right to the hotel. The Mercedes he had stored on the street behind the Argyle house would eventually be found abandoned in the parking lot of the Galleria mall.

He checked his reflection in the mirror and smiled. "When a door closes, look for an open window."

Gant and his legion of idiots would never in their lifetimes uncover all his assets. As he'd driven away from the hotel he'd toyed with the idea of leaving now and returning to his home in Bangkok. *Not yet.* His fingers tightened on the steering wheel. He would finish this. By the time he took his leave this city would never forget his name. This sweltering, murderous summer would be forever emblazoned on its history.

He'd been forced to rethink his strategy, but his goal remained the same. This was the first step toward that end. It had been a great while since he'd carried out such menial tasks personally. He'd grown rather selective over the years. Nonetheless, the ability to adapt was quite priceless at a time like this.

The game had changed, yes, but the objectives had not. Jess's turn would come. First however, he wanted to ensure Burnett suffered, excruciatingly so. He wanted the man to rue the day he was born. Originally, he'd intended to merely kill Burnett, but then he'd realized that spending the rest of his life in agony was by far the more fitting punishment. Eric wondered why he hadn't done this already. The simplistic beauty of the move was one of unreserved brilliance.

Burnett had shattered Eric's meticulous plans. He had charged into the house Eric had so carefully prepared and taken everything…well, almost everything. Whatever else happened he still had one shocking move to make. He wished he could be there to see the look on Burnett's face. By the end of this day, Burnett would be asking himself how things could possibly get any worse. *If only he knew.*

Relishing the anticipation, Eric checked the street again before emerging from the car. He strolled to the other side and up the sidewalk, admiring the landscape as he approached the door. At the last possible moment, he changed course and headed to the rear of the house. Rusty or not, the hunt was much like the kill itself—one never forgot the rhythm.

He paused at a window near the kitchen entrance. Daniel Burnett, Senior, sat in a chair at the table. As Eric watched, he bent down and tied the laces of first one shoe and then the other. Golfing shoes. Mr. Burnett had an afternoon on the green planned, did he? It was such a shame he wouldn't be able to make it. A good game of golf was cathartic.

Eric reached for the door. He smiled as the knob turned without resistance. These southerners were such trusting souls. He was in the kitchen and standing next to the older man before he could do more than rise from his chair.

Eric plunged the needle into his neck. "Hello, Mr. Burnett."

The man staggered back, knocking over his chair and causing the table to shake, rattling the cup and saucer there.

"Now, now, let's not break anything. I'm certain the little missus would be quite upset." Eric selected a couple of nicely sharpened knives from a drawer, and then he took the old man by the arm and ushered him into the hallway. "Let's get you to bed, Mr. Burnett."

By the time they reached the master bedroom Burnett could hardly stand. Eric propped him on the end of the bed and began removing his clothes. A man should leave the world the same way he came into it.

Burnett struggled to cry out or to speak, but he couldn't quite vocalize the sounds.

"It's the drug," Eric assured him. "Speech is difficult at this dosage." Eric surveyed the failing muscle tone and sagging skin. "Ah, the devastating effects of time." He pulled the old man into a supine position on the bed. "While we play shall I tell you about my plans for your son?"

Those faded blue eyes rounded with terror as if he'd only just realized the identity of his unexpected visitor.

"That's right, Mr. Burnett. My name is Eric Spears and I'm here to take your life, but first, I'll share with you what I have in store for Dan." The notion of dissecting the father had Eric fully aroused. This was the first time in more than a decade he'd made a spur of the moment kill.

Eric tugged gloves firmly into place and chose his instrument. A nice, razor sharp paring knife. A minute insertion exactly positioned between the nipples and crimson appeared. The first bloom of blood was always the most exciting. Burnett whimpered and cried like a child. Eric slid the tip of the blade from breastbone to navel, opening only a few layers of flesh. The rush of blood made him even harder.

"I'm going to disembowel your son first," Eric explained. "I assure you he will feel every sweep of the scalpel. Then, I'll move on to his genitals. He won't need them, after all. Then, if he's very lucky, help will arrive before it's too late. He'll spend the rest of his life dumping his own waste from a plastic bag."

The old man's body shuddered and shook as if he were having a seizure. Eric leaned close to make sure he heard the rest. "After that, I'm going to have Jess all to myself. That little grandchild of yours budding inside her will die with her."

Burnett's body stiffened.

Eric reared back. "Now, now, we can't have that."

The choking and gasping came next. The man was having a cardiac episode. Eric pounded a fist into his flailing cnest. "I am not finished with you!"

Burnett's body shuddered again before going still.

Eric roared like a wounded animal with the rage gushing through him. He stormed across the room, turned, and retraced his steps. "What now? What now?"

He stalled, stretched his neck to relieve the tension, and then adjusted the lapels of his silk jacket. "Very well. Have it your way."

Eric strode back to the bed and placed his gloved hand on the man's unnaturally still chest. He counted down to just the right set of ribs above the heart. He selected the long-bladed knife, poised it, and prepared to drive it into the failing organ.

Raised voices and laughter jerked his head up.

Outside. *Close.* Females.

Eric walked to the nearest window and checked the street. He counted five cars parked in front of the house and five...six...seven women headed toward the front door.

More of that blinding wrath swept through him. He glanced back at the dying man and clenched his fists in fury.

This was unacceptable.

His options limited, Eric slipped out the back door as the horde of bitches flooded in through the front. When he'd settled behind the wheel of the car, he powered down the window and started the engine.

Screams filled the air as he drove away.

CHAPTER TEN

Dolly North Beecham's hands trembled before she could clasp them together and halt the outward indicator of just how nervous she was.

"Ms. Beecham, you are not in any sort of trouble," Jess assured her. "We simply need to ask you a few questions about your brother, Quentin."

Beecham heaved a big breath. "I knew he was up to something. He quit work about two months ago and bought a new car. I worried he'd gotten involved with drugs again."

Interesting. "Quentin had no criminal record. In what way was he involved with drugs? Did he have an addiction?"

The woman shook her head. "He never used drugs at all. Not even back in high school. A few years ago, when the office where he worked closed, he turned to selling drugs to survive. His wife left him. His whole life went to hell. Even after all that he managed to get back on his feet and seemed to be doing fine."

Jess didn't miss the underlying doubt in her voice. "But you weren't so sure everything was fine."

"I know my brother. Whenever things appear too good to be true they usually are. Deep down, he was a good guy. Or he used to be."

Jess wasn't so sure Beecham knew her brother as well as she thought. "What changed?"

"Everything." She shrugged. "Maybe nothing really. No matter how hard he worked his life always fell apart. He never had any decent luck with women. They were always cruel to him, but to hear them tell it he was the bully. If he bought a car it turned out to be a lemon. His coworkers always picked on him. He was bullied as a kid in school. It was the story of his life. If it wasn't for bad luck, he wouldn't have had any at all." She scrubbed at her damp eyes with her fists. "I was the only person who ever really consistently cared about him."

"What about your parents?"

Beecham harrumphed. "The old man beat Quentin every chance he got. Momma died when we were little kids. Life was not easy for either of us."

"Had you noticed anything different about Quentin since he bought his new car? Had he mentioned anyone new in his life?"

"The only thing he said to me was that I should be very proud of him. He had a new job, though he wouldn't say where and what kind, and he insisted that everyone was going to find out just how important he was. He claimed he had a lot of new friends and that he was going to be a big star."

Jess sat up a little straighter. "Do you remember the names of any of his new friends?"

Beecham shook her head. "He never mentioned their names."

Lori stepped into the living room and took a seat on the sofa next to Jess. She gave a small shake of her head. Beecham had given authorization for Lori to have a look in the garage since North had gone in there a couple of times when he'd visited over the past month.

"Mrs. Beecham, if you think of anything else please call me." Jess extended a card across the coffee table. "Day or night."

Beecham studied the card, a frown lining her brow. "You know, he didn't mention any names, but he did text me photos of him and some of his new friends." She managed a halfhearted smile. "Mostly women. I guess he figured out how to be a bit of a Casanova after all. He always said he wanted to be one of those guys women would do anything for. Some of 'em look pretty desperate to me, if you know what I mean."

Jess's pulse rate sped up. "May I see the photos?"

"Sure." Beecham reached for the cell phone on the table next to her chair, and then stood. "I swear, if it wasn't for texting I probably wouldn't have heard a word from him except when he wanted to get in the garage. People don't have real conversations anymore. I guess his new job was keeping him busy."

Beecham came around to the sofa and sat down on the other side of Jess. "Let's see here." She tapped the necessary keys until she reached her text messages. "Here you go." She passed the phone to Jess. "Feel free to look at anything you want."

The first photo was of North and Amanda Brownfield. Amanda had her arms around him and was smiling. Jess's instincts started to hum. The date accompanying the text was mid July.

Jess stalled on the next photo.

Meredith Dority.

Meredith looked more than desperate, she looked terrified. North held her tight against him in the *selfie* he'd snapped no doubt only minutes before murdering her.

Beecham had replied, asking her brother if this was his new girlfriend and when he was going to come and visit his lonely sister. Jess scrolled to the next photo.

Nina Baron.

Wearing a yellow nightgown, she sat in a chair in a darkened room. North had crouched next to the chair and snapped the pic. Nina looked disoriented and terrified. Jess tried to make out any other elements of the room but it was too dark.

"I'll call Chief Burnett," Lori offered.

"We need North's cell phone records." Jess scrolled back to the photo of Nina. "This text was sent just yesterday. Wherever this photo was taken, Nina might still be there."

"I'll see if we can't bypass the usual delays," Lori said, reading Jess's mind.

"We have cause," Jess agreed. North was dead and Nina Baron's kidnapping provided extenuating circumstances. Jess turned to North's sister. "We're going to need to keep your cell phone for evidence. Is that all right? I'll gladly buy you a new one to use until we're finished."

Beecham shrugged. "Whatever you need."

"Detective Wells, let's get Mrs. Beecham's phone to Ricky Vernon at the lab." Jess's pulse bumped into a faster rhythm. "He may be able to give us the time as well as the location from each of the photos."

"I'll call," Lori agreed, "and let him know we're en route."

Jess's cell rang. *Dan calling.* "Excuse me for just one moment." Jess dug for her phone as she moved toward the kitchen for privacy. "Hey, what's up?"

"It's Dad."

Jess stilled at the sound of his voice, her heart dipping. "What's happened?"

"He had a heart attack. We're at UAB."

"I'll be right there." Jess's throat was so tight she could hardly get the words out.

"It was Spears, Jess. He went to my parents' house and tortured my father…"

"Katherine?"

"Thank God she wasn't home."

"I'm on my way, Dan." Jess put her phone away and went in search of Lori.

"I got Chief Burnett's voicemail—" Lori started to explain.

"He's at the ER. His father had a heart attack."

"Is Mr. Burnett okay?"

Jess shook her head. "I'm not sure. We need to get to the hospital."

UAB HOSPITAL. BIRMINGHAM. 3:10 P.M.

Jess rushed from the elevator, Lori right on her heels, and went straight to the nurse's desk of the Cardiac Unit. "Can you direct me to the family waiting room?"

"Around the corner to your left, second door on the right." The nurse glanced at Lori then back to Jess. "There's a larger waiting area in the first floor lobby."

Jess thanked her but didn't bother explaining that Lori had refused to wait downstairs as suggested by the information desk. Like the rest of her team, she wasn't allowing Jess out of her sight—not even to take Beecham's cell phone to the lab.

At the door to the family waiting room, Lori paused. "I'll head to the lab now, and then I'll be back for you."

Jess nodded, the reality of why they were *here* hitting her all over again. "Call me the second Vernon has something. And let Black and Gant know as well."

"On it." Lori rushed back to the elevators.

Jess drew in a deep breath and opened the door. Dan looked up from his chair and Jess felt sick at the worry and fear she saw on his face. Katherine's eyes were red from crying. Dan patted his mother's hand and stood.

Jess hurried to him and hugged him with all her might. What if his father died? That would be her fault, too. She couldn't bear it. When she was reasonably sure she could speak, she drew back and searched Dan's eyes. *So much sadness and all her fault.* "How is he?"

"We don't know yet. The doctor's determining the damage now. From there, he'll make a decision on the course of action to take."

Feeling unsteady, Jess took the seat on the other side of Katherine and wrapped her hands around her future mother-in-law's.

Dan settled back into his seat. "Mom was able to see him a few minutes ago."

Katherine dabbed at her eyes. "He's better. I think. He swears he's going to be fine, but he wouldn't tell me if he thought he was dying." Her voice cracked. "They're checking that stint he had to have four years ago. The doctor said he might need another one."

Jess put her arm around Katherine's shoulders. "He couldn't be in better hands." Birmingham's UAB hospital was one of the best in the nation. Dan placed his arm over hers and smiled sadly. Jess wanted to hug him and ask him what on earth happened, but she didn't want to upset Katherine any more than she already was.

"Why don't I get some coffee?" Dan suggested.

"That would be wonderful, son. Two sugars, please." Katherine heaved a burdened breath. "I just can't believe it."

Dan stood and Jess started to as well, but Katherine held onto her hand. "Please stay with me, Jess."

Jess looked to Dan and then back to Katherine. "Of course." She eased back into her seat. "I'll stay right here."

When Dan had gone, Jess and Katherine had the small room to themselves. Katherine rambled on about how she'd been urging Dan Senior to go for his check up. Jess smiled and nodded on cue.

"I'm sure Dan will tell you what happened later." Katherine tightened her hold on Jess's hand. "He doesn't want to talk about it in front of me." Her lips trembled into a smile. "He wants to protect me, but there's no need to make you wait. I saw what that devil did to him."

Jess kept her mouth shut. If Katherine wanted to talk, she would be glad to listen, but she wasn't asking a single thing. She refused to be responsible for upsetting Dan's mother at a time like this.

"I was having lunch with my friends. Shirley, my oldest friend in the world, just finagled millions in a divorce from her second husband. She's planning on redecorating her house and she wanted my advice."

"She's a smart lady." Jess knew Katherine's decorating style. While it wasn't her own, there was no denying the woman had talent. Especially if it meant she was able to spend big money on expensive things. *That was a bad thought, Jess.* She really was working hard at only having good thoughts about Dan's mother. Not always easy.

"Dan Senior was going golfing. He insisted the nice young man from the department go with me." She frowned. "I shouldn't have left him alone." She looked at Jess then. "*He* came into our home."

"This isn't you fault," Jess said, offering the only comfort she could.

"I don't know exactly what happened." Katherine put a hand to her throat. "But that devil stripped my Dan's clothes from him and cut him all the while telling him all these awful things he was going to do to our son."

"He's a monster." Jess wanted Spears to rot in hell. She wanted to be the one who put the bullet in his brain.

"It was nothing but a pure miracle." She glanced heavenward. "The waiting time at the restaurant was forty-five minutes so the girls and I decided to go back to my house." Katherine made a sound, a sort of keening. "I found him in the bedroom. He wasn't breathing. Shirley, bless her heart, started CPR while I fell to pieces. She saved his life, I'm certain."

"I'm so sorry, Katherine." Jess fought back the tears.

Katherine turned to her. "I need you to promise me something, Jess."

"I'm glad to help any way I can." There was no way to make up for the pain she'd brought this family.

"When you get him and I know you will…"

Jess appreciated the vote of confidence, but at this point she wasn't sure of anything anymore. Spears was changing the game at every turn. "I'll do my best," she assured Katherine.

"I want you to kill him, Jess. Don't let him end up in some mental institution or prison somewhere. *Kill him.* Do you hear me? Kill that devil so he never has the chance to hurt us or anyone else ever again."

Dan returned just then, preventing Jess from having to make a promise she might not be able to keep.

Promise or no promise, first she had to catch the son of a bitch. Whether he was scrambling for a new plan of action or simply coming apart at the seams, he could suddenly decide to cut his losses and disappear.

A terrible sinking feeling tugged at her. If Spears vanished…she'd be looking over her shoulder the rest of her life.

CHAPTER ELEVEN

"I'm certainly glad to hear your father is recovering." Frank Teller shook his head. "Damn, Dan, you just can't catch a break lately, though I have to say the photos found on Quentin North's phone—particularly the one of him and Dority—could prove helpful. I'm pushing Chief Black to see that photo as evidence she was still alive when you left her home. The issue is timing. Proving when you arrived and when you left." Teller heaved a sigh. "I have every confidence we'll get there."

Dan had no intention of admitting the truth to Frank or to anyone else. Yesterday had almost gotten the better of him. Despite the potential break in Meredith's case, the ever-present threat from Eric Spears was more than enough to push the strongest man to the edge. Mayor Joseph Pratt had cut off all communications with Dan. The man had groomed him for the position of chief of police for years and then turned on him for doing his job. It was amazing the lengths some people would go to in the name of power. Dan scrubbed a hand over his face. The Ted Allen case was more of the same. The man had gone missing weeks ago and Dan was the only person of interest they had in his disappearance. Then his dad was tortured and had a heart attack—more of Spears' doing.

How the hell was he supposed to handle all that at once?

Because there was no other choice. Jess and their baby were counting on him.

"I'm fine," Dan lied to his old friend and attorney. "So what happens next as far as the Internal Affairs investigation goes?" At the moment, that was the most pressing issue. IAB had the power to clear him of misconduct in the performance of his duties as chief of police so he could return to work. Dan didn't want Harold getting too attached to the position.

Jess needed to see him strong and in control. Her strength and determination continually amazed him. He was so damned lucky to have her back in his life. How had he ever hoped to live without her?

"Anne Colbert is the lead investigator on your IA case."

Dan considered the news. "I'm not familiar with the name."

"She's a transplant to the department from Boston and she's tough as they come. The bright side of having her assigned to your case is that if you're telling the truth she will find the facts that clear you." Frank turned his hands up. "If you're holding anything back or not being completely honest she will nail your ass to the wall. Now is the time to give it to me straight, Dan. If there's anything she can find on you that I don't know already we need to talk about it and find a way to spin it to our advantage."

Dan shook his head. "How many times do I have to tell you, I haven't done anything wrong? I sure as hell didn't kill Meredith or Allen. As for the years I served as liaison between the mayor and the BPD, Pratt is twisting things around to make me look bad when I was the one who kept him out of hot water." He let go a heavy breath. "Pratt has a penchant for using his position to achieve what he wants and to help out his friends. None of his transgressions are earth shattering, but they're enough to get him thrown out of office."

"Unfortunately," Frank allowed, "that issue boils down to one thing, your word against his. Right now that's not a good thing."

"What are we doing to change that?" Dan was tired of hearing about his problems. He wanted to discuss solutions.

"Right now, you and I are going to spend a couple of hours prepping you for Colbert. Meanwhile, my investigators are out there beating the bushes looking for answers."

None of which made Dan feel any better as to how this would end. "Before we begin," Dan needed to confirm he'd taken all the right steps...just in case, "I've made Jess the beneficiary for all my life insurance plans, pensions, investments, and so forth. The will outlining my wishes regarding my estate has been taken care of. Is there anything else I should do to ensure she and the baby are taken care of in the event of my death?"

"This Spears creep is really getting to you."

Since the statement was a rhetorical one, Dan didn't bother to confirm the allegation. "Jess and the baby are my top priorities."

Frank shrugged. "You've squared away all the usual legal matters with my colleague at our office. The only other thing that would benefit Jess is for the two of you to tie the knot before any untimely departure on your part."

"That's not going to happen." Dan laughed. "Between my parents and Jess's sister, there has to be a wedding."

Frank laughed. "I'll bet Katherine has already reserved a date at St. Paul's."

"She has. Just don't tell Jess. I'm staying out of that one. If my mother can convince Jess to have a full-blown Catholic wedding I'll go along just to make her happy. If it was up to me, we'd get married in the courthouse today."

Frank leaned forward and picked up his note-pad. "Well then, let's get to it."

Dan readied to face whatever his old friend would throw his way.

10:15 A.M.

Dan walked out into the bright sunlight, grateful the grilling session with Frank was over. He nodded to the officers providing his surveillance today. Now he understood what Jess hated so much about being watched. It was more than a little frustrating.

He climbed into his rental and started the engine to get the air conditioning going. It was hot as hell. Besides buying a house, he needed to take the time to find a new car. He was leaning toward another Mercedes SUV, principally for the endless safety features available on the new models. Maybe he'd buy Jess one, too. That ten-year-old Audi of hers was not so child friendly.

Rather than pull away from the curb he took a moment to make a call he'd been debating for two days. His plan was a risky maneuver, but at this point he was desperate enough to take the risk. He had to protect Jess and the baby at all costs. It was more than apparent that Spears wasn't backing off. A wise man would have disappeared by now. If he was caught, he would never see the light of day again. Yet, for some insane reason— insane being the operative word—he just wouldn't stop this taunting game he was playing with Jess.

His relentless determination scared the hell out of Dan. Since Spears had the means to keep himself off the grid catching him seemed next to impossible. Unless he screwed up. They'd caught a break on Friday, saving the lives of three hostages. They might not get that lucky again.

Dan wasn't waiting for luck. He had to do something.

He hit the contact name and made the call. When Buddy Corlew answered, Dan almost ended the call, but he didn't. He had to do this. "We need to talk."

"Danny boy," Corlew enthused, "what do you want to talk about?"

As if he didn't know. "I'm confident you don't need me to spell it out for you."

"How can I help?"

Dan hesitated for only a moment before saying what needed to be said. "If I provide you with Spears's contact number—"

"This sounds like something you should run by Jess first."

Irritation twisted in Dan's gut. "I need you to set up a meeting with Spears."

Corlew laughed, and Dan wished they were face to face so he could kick his ass. "If it was that simple, why hasn't Gant or someone done it already? You gotta get real, Danny boy, Spears had a bad day but he's no fool."

"I have something he wants."

The silence extended for five, then ten seconds.

"And what's that?" Corlew asked, his voice suddenly devoid of emotion.

"*Me.*"

CHAPTER TWELVE

See what you made me do. Everything is wrong...

Jess had received the call she had hoped wouldn't come. Presley Campbell's body had been found.

Evidence techs were swarming the warehouse. There was an additional bloody area besides the one where Campbell's body was positioned. The fire ax left on the floor next to the second bloody mess was likely where Quentin North had met his demise. Forensic techs would check for Nina Baron's blood type to ensure she hadn't been here.

"Dammit," Jess muttered. One dead and another still missing.

The old warehouse hadn't been used in years, the wear of time and neglect served as a morbid backdrop to the vicious murders. The young victim lay on a wooden table, her legs and arms tied wide apart. In Jess's estimation she had been dead for at least twenty-four hours.

Jess reminded herself to breathe through her mouth. The warehouse was like an oven. The accelerated stench of decomposition was overwhelming.

She had seen Spears's work first hand many times. He was methodical, precise, and infinitely ruthless. He had studied the human body. Each carefully placed assault was chosen to wield the most pain. He always took his time, relishing each move and drawing out his pleasure.

Not with this victim. Presley Campbell's body had been slashed repeatedly with a ferocity that spoke of rage and an inability to maintain control. She had been raped over and over. Her breasts had practically been ripped from her body. When he'd finished, he'd stabbed her over and over.

"He lost control." The idea of how this woman must have suffered in those last minutes of her life tore at Jess.

"He's never done this to a victim before?" Lori asked quietly.

Jess shook her head. "At least not since he was dubbed the Player and landed on the Bureau's radar."

"You really think he's losing it?"

Jess thought of the way he'd barged into Dan Senior's house and attacked him like a novice just starting to hone his technique, and then running away when interrupted rather than killing anyone who got in his way. Now this. "If this is his work, he's unraveling at breakneck speed."

"You think it might be a new rookie follower? Kind of reminds me of Reed's unfocused work."

Lori was right. Matthew Reed had left a similar scene. His work had been scattered and frantic. This had the same feel.

Jess weighed the concept. "Possibly, but many of the wounds are classic Player. The idea that he turned a hostage over to a follower to finish off is totally out of character." Not to mention, Dan Senior had positively identified Spears.

"Unless he's gone."

Lori's words echoed in Jess's soul as she stared at the message left on the wall, most likely in this woman's blood. *See what you made me do. Everything is wrong....*

"No." Jess shook her head. "He's here and he's madder than hell that we got in his way." Or, maybe he really was losing it. The thought sent chills through Jess. If he went on a rampage, how many people would be slaughtered before they caught him?

News from the lab hadn't been as helpful as Jess had hoped. Ricky Vernon had confirmed the times and dates the selfies were taken by North. Unfortunately, the location services of the phone had been disabled so Vernon wasn't able to access the GPS coordinates of where the photos had been taken. The photo with Meredith had been taken during the estimated timeframe of her death, but that alone wouldn't clear Dan. The one with Nina had been taken late the night she disappeared, confirming who took her without telling them where she was being held. *Dammit.*

Hopefully, North's cell carrier would have something for them this morning.

Toni James and a morgue tech arrived with a body bag and a gurney. Jess pushed aside her frustrations and focused on the here and now. She opted not to nudge James about time of death. This one was going to be tough enough without any flak from Jess.

"Chief?"

Jess turned to Harper who was striding her way. "Did you find something?"

"I got a call from North's cell carrier."

"Something we can use, I hope."

"The guy was smart enough to turn off the location services on his phone, but I guess he didn't realize if he sent a text it could be retrieved by his carrier. He sent his location to a burner phone right before he sent his sister the pic of Nina Baron. No hits on the burner phone, but we do have the address where Nina was being held at that time."

Anticipation chased away the chill nagging at Jess. "Let's go."

"We've got backup headed that way," Hayes assured her as he joined Harper. "They'll be in position in twenty minutes.

Jess wasn't waiting for backup. If there was any chance at all Nina Baron was still at that location, Jess intended to find her.

MASONIC TEMPLE BUILDING. 4TH AVENUE.
10:52 A.M.

The old building had been abandoned since the 80's and had fallen into serious disrepair.

"We should wait until the other team is in place," Harper urged. "We don't know what we'll run into in there."

"How much more time do they need?" Jess wanted to go in now. There were eight or nine floors not counting the basement, a lot of territory to cover and endless possibilities for hiding.

"They're ready now," Hayes confirmed.

"Bout time," Jess grumbled. She tightened her bulletproof vest over the soft pink jacket dress she'd chosen for today and palmed her Glock. "Let's move in. I want through those doors the instant an all clear is called on the basement and the first floor."

Jess and Lori took a position near the front entrance. Harper and Hayes moved around to the rear. As Jess considered all those stairs she was grateful for her new, more practical shoes. The lower heeled Mary Janes were working out well. Something else she'd had to learn to live with. The joys of pregnancy included rethinking her entire wardrobe. And she'd only just begun.

The all clear on the basement and first level sounded in the earpiece of Jess's communications link and she and Lori moved in.

Once inside, Jess opted to have a look at the basement level first. In the photo North had taken it had been the kind of dark found in rooms with no windows.

"Let's go down first," she said to Lori.

Lori nodded and led the way. Flashlight in hand, Jess scanned the walls for messages and the steps and floor for dropped items. The basement level smelled musty. The area was cluttered with tables and chairs from the years the building was a public library.

The occasional swish of scurrying feet and tails across the floor warned that rats had made the place home. Jess wondered if Spears had borrowed a few from here to load into North's mouth. The vermin had been basically trapped until the assistant coroner had opened the vic's mouth far enough for them to scramble out.

Jess shuddered. Not that she felt sorry for North. She didn't.

"Over here," Lori called.

Careful of the cracks that left the concrete floor uneven, Jess made her way to Lori's position. She roved the beam of her flashlight over the wooden chair sitting apart from the rest of the stored goods.

"This is the place." Jess didn't have to check the image of Nina she'd forwarded to herself from Beecham's cell phone.

The chair sat alone in a small, uncluttered space. The ropes used to bind Nina's hands and feet lay on the floor. Why hadn't Spears sent Jess a message about Nina? Why hadn't she been at the Argyle Drive house?

Was it possible that North had taken Nina on his own?

No. This was Spears. Jess was certain of it.

"At least we know who we're dealing with now," Lori said.

That much was true. They could rule out an abduction motivated by ransom or the theory of negligence on the part of the clinic's staff. Nina Baron hadn't just walked away. She'd been taken by the worst kind of killer—one too smart to get caught.

"Let's get the forensic folks over here."

Whatever was happening inside Eric Spears's head, it looked as if he had one strategic move left.

Nina Baron was in grave danger.

BIRMINGHAM POLICE DEPARTMENT, 2:30 P.M.

Harper busily scribbled notes on the timeline of their case board. Hayes had left early to drop by the hospital and visit Cook. Jess didn't want Cook feeling out of the loop. She wanted him to know he was still part of the team no matter that he was stuck in the hospital. Hopefully by Friday he would be out of ICU.

Evidence reports were in. Not a single print belonging to Spears had been discovered at the Argyle Drive house. No evidence at all that connected to him. The same was true for the Infiniti where North's body was found. Jess didn't need a crystal ball to know it would be the same for the scenes at the Burnett home and at the abandoned warehouse. Spears never left an evidence trail.

Jess had spoken to Gant about her theory that Spears was unraveling. The signs had started with the discovery of the Argyle Drive house. Amanda Brownfield had thrown a wrench in the works. She had set off a chain reaction of failures. Spears was not taking it well. Rather than walk away while he still could, he appeared determined to prove his superior intelligence would allow him to win and to escape as he had been doing for years. He wasn't thinking clearly. Whether his deterioration would prove advantageous to their efforts was yet to be seen.

Another thought occurred to Jess. Maybe he'd started to come undone months ago when he decided to focus so completely on her.

"I just got Reverend Henshaw's phone records!" Lori tapped a few keys on her computer keyboard and the printer on the other side of the room hummed to life. "I'll start comparing numbers to see if he was contacted by North or Spears or anyone else of interest."

"We can hope." The phone on Jess's desk rang. She jumped. Most people called her cell. It was rare that she received a call on the landline at her desk. "Maybe because you're rarely here," she mused as she picked up the handset. "Harris."

"Chief Harris, this is Sheila."

Dan's secretary. Jess despised the idea that Black was using not only Dan's office, but also his personnel. "Hey, Sheila. I'm sorry, I should have called you about Dan's father." She'd promised Dan she would keep everyone at work updated. "He's out of the woods now and should be able to go home on Wednesday or Thursday."

"That's wonderful news." Sheila sounded immensely relieved. There was a moment of silence before she cleared her throat. "I was calling to ask if you're available. Chief Black would like to see you for a few moments."

Jess considered saying she was on her way out the door. She imagined this was why Black had instructed Sheila to call on the department landline. Jess couldn't say she was out of the office.

"Absolutely. I'll be right up."

Jess placed the handset in the cradle and reached for her bag. "I have a meeting with the acting chief of police." Both Lori and Harper looked unimpressed. "I'll be back shortly. I hope."

By the time she reached the door, Harper was right behind her. "I'll tag along in case Black needs protection."

"Ha ha," Jess replied. Actually, Harper wasn't far off base.

As they strode toward the stairwell, Harper asked, "You think this might have something to do with that *selfie* of North and Dority?"

"Considering the carrier was able to pinpoint the location as her neighborhood, I suppose it's possible."

"The photo has to carry some weight regardless. We know North was working for Spears. We know he killed Henshaw and the three vics in Jackson County—all were shown in those creepy *selfies* he took. It doesn't take much of a leap to conclude he killed Dority, too."

"That's the only theory that makes any kind of sense," Jess agreed. "The question is, will the DA or the Grand Jury see it that way?"

"I'm hoping the case won't make it that far."

"Me and you both, Sergeant."

Harper opened the door into the Chief of Police's suite of offices. Jess remembered the first time she'd walked through these doors after returning to Birmingham. Had it only been a little over two months ago? She'd been nervous about seeing Dan face to face again after so many years, and yet, she'd had no other choice. He'd needed her to help with a case and her career at the Bureau was in the toilet. She'd needed a break. Coming here and helping him had felt like the right thing to do. At the time, she really hadn't thought of Birmingham as home.

Now, she couldn't imagine home as anyplace else.

Tara, the receptionist, wasn't at her desk so Jess and Harper continued on to Sheila's desk.

"Hey, Sheila." Jess pushed a smile into place.

Sheila's smile was wide and genuine. She skirted her desk and gave Jess a hug. As she drew back, her smile fell. "He said you should come on in when you arrive." She glanced back at Harper. "I think he wants to see you alone."

Jess winked at Harper. "I brought the Sergeant along to keep you company."

Sheila giggled. "In that case the next few minutes will be the best part of my day."

Jess headed into Dan's office. She absolutely refused to refer to the space as Black's. Sheila was already offering refreshments to Harper. Jess took a breath and opened the door. Black looked up as she entered.

"Chief Harris, I'm glad you had time to see me."

Jess took a seat in front of Dan's desk and set her bag on the floor. "Would you like a personal update on what we found at the Masonic Temple building?"

He held up his hands. "That won't be necessary. I have Detective Wells's report and I've already been briefed about the findings at the Temple by a member of the advance entry team."

"So, what can I do for you today?" She did have work to do.

"Harris, I owe you an apology."

Jess almost asked him to repeat himself.

"I didn't get the message about the operation at the Argyle Drive house because I was at a doctor's appointment with my wife. I don't usually shut off my phone, but I did for that one."

"I hope it's nothing serious."

"It's cancer, Harris. Lung cancer, stage four. The prognosis is not good."

"I'm sorry." She shook her head. God, what did she say? "I'm really sorry."

"Funny thing is she's never smoked a cigarette in her life. Neither have I. It just doesn't make sense."

Jess understood. Sometimes life didn't make sense at all.

"As you've probably noticed I haven't been myself for awhile."

"Completely understandable," she assured him.

"I do want to reiterate my concern about what happened at Argyle Drive."

And here she'd thought he was going to let it go. "I'm listening."

"Dan is on administrative leave right now. Allowing him to enter a scene, much less to participate in an investigation, is asking for trouble, Harris. I understand he was at the Sloss Furnaces scene as well. I'm certain you're aware of the proper protocols."

"The situation at the Argyle Drive house was an unusual one. That said, I do believe Chief Burnett removed himself from the scene as soon as you arrived. As for the Sloss Furnaces scene he was my ride and, frankly, Dan knows the area better than anyone else who was available at the time. His help was needed."

"Those are all valid points." Black leaned back in his chair and steepled his fingers in front of him. "I don't want to sound as if I'm pushing Dan away. I'm only trying to protect him. This isn't the wild, wild west, Harris. We have laws to follow. Dan is facing enough trouble right now. We both need to do all we can to ensure he steers clear of any other potential issues."

She couldn't argue with his reasoning. "I'll see that it doesn't happen again." She stood. "Anything else?"

"I appreciate your support, Harris. We both want Dan back in this office."

Jess hoped that was true. "I hope you'll let us know if there's anything we can do to help, Chief." The news about his wife was devastating.

"Pray. That's all we can do now."

On the way out Jess promised to keep Sheila posted. Once she and Harper were in the stairwell, Jess exhaled a weary breath. "Remind me to start making an effort to be nice to Chief Black."

Harper laughed. "We should mark this day on the calendar then."

"Maybe so, Sergeant."

Once they were back on the third floor, Jess relaxed a little. "Let's see if Lori found something useful in Henshaw's phone records."

Harper opened the door to the SPU office for Jess to enter before him. "Give us something good, Lori."

"Do I count?"

Jess stalled. "Sylvia." Was there news about Nina?

Sylvia must have read the question on her face. "No news. I just stopped by to thank you for finding the connection between Spears and Nina. That's something."

Jess nodded. "We understand what we're up against."

Sylvia bit her lower lip when it trembled. "I know you'll do all you can."

"I will."

"I saw Dan's father today. He's doing great."

"He is. It was a little scary there for a minute, but he's going to be fine." Jess was incredibly thankful. She wasn't sure she could bear it if Dan lost his father at all, much less because of her. Besides, their child needed both of his or her grandparents.

"I have some other news for you," Sylvia said quietly.

Jess ushered Sylvia to her desk. "The test results are in?"

Sylvia nodded.

Jess felt her knees go a little weak. The questions about her father and who he really was that had come to light last week had shaken Jess and Lily's worlds. Learning they had a half sister, Amanda Brownfield, had proven another stunner. But Spears hadn't been through playing games with Jess even then. He'd led her to a twisted taxidermist up in Jackson County who for years had been stealing all sorts of human body parts from a local funeral home. Among his preserved treasures Jess had found a fetus Spears wanted her to believe was taken from her mother after her death.

"Maybe we should sit down," Sylvia suggested.

"Sure." Jess leaned against her desk while Sylvia took the chair in front of it. "Was my mother pregnant when she died?"

Sylvia shook her head. "The DNA wasn't a match. Wherever the fetus came from, it wasn't from your mother or anyone else genetically connected to you."

Relief washed over Jess. The idea that the baby might have been removed from her mother by a fiend not unlike Eric Spears had sickened Jess. Still, it had happened to someone. The Alabama Bureau of Investigation and the FBI were investigating the Brownfield body farm as well as the criminal activity at the funeral home.

"Thank you for letting me know. It gives me hope that if Spears lied about that for the shock value he could be lying about a lot more."

Sylvia nodded. "We have to stop him, Jess."

"He's changing the game, scrambling for purchase. I'm hoping he'll screw up badly enough to get caught any minute now."

"Finding three of his hostages alive gives me hope," Sylvia admitted. "For Nina."

It gave Jess hope for all of them. She could barely remember what her life was like before Spears. She had made a promise to her child that he or she would never so much as know the name. There was only one way to keep that promise.

Spears had to die.

CHAPTER THIRTEEN

"Thank you so much for rescuing me from work." Jess leaned across the console and gave Dan a kiss. She was relatively certain that was a first. No one had ever dared to suggest she should leave work early, much less showed up with a puppy in tow to take her away. Even more surprising, she'd said yes.

The truth was, after finding Presley Campbell's body, hearing such painful news from Black, and then learning there was nothing in Henshaw's phone records that helped their investigation, Jess had been more than ready to call it a day. Sharing the awful news about Black's wife with Dan had been the final straw.

As if reading her mind, Dan sent her an understanding smile. "We both needed a break."

From the backseat, the puppy stretched up on his hind legs to lick Dan's jaw. Jess laughed. "I think you might be his favorite."

Dan reached for the leash. The puppy seemed to comprehend what that meant. He started to bounce. "I think he's taken with the both of us."

"It's hard to believe we have our first pet together." It was way outside her comfort zone, but if she could have a baby, she could certainly have a family pet.

"Assuming Linda doesn't find one of those chips that proves he belongs to someone else."

"True." Jess wasn't sure how she felt about potentially losing the puppy. She almost laughed at herself. The nesting instinct had taken over!

While Dan wrangled the puppy, Jess climbed out. She and Cook had done all they could to find the puppy's owner after the loveable animal had showed up a few days ago. They'd had no luck. Having Dan's veterinarian friend check for a chip and give the puppy a routine examination was the next step. If there was no chip, they could officially claim him.

The Happy Pets Clinic was bright and colorful with a friendly staff. Jess surveyed the numerous pet food brands. She had no idea what was considered the best for growing puppies. All these years she'd been totally focused on work. It seemed she was playing catch up on all the domestic responsibilities she'd ignored for decades. She'd spent several nights now poring over *What to Expect When You're Expecting*—a gift from Lily. Dan had picked up a book about a puppy's first year. Here they were in their forties and scrambling to learn what to do next. They needed a reality show. She doubted any of the other popular shows had their own serial killer. Not exactly the best kind of bragging rights. She shuddered.

"You okay?"

Jess glanced up at the man with whom she intended to spend the rest of her life. "Yes. I'm very okay. I just don't know about dog foods or parasite protection." Puppies needed a lot of care, just like babies.

Dan grinned. "We'll see what Linda thinks is best."

"Sounds good to me." She was planning to do the same thing with the baby. Lil was her walking, talking baby bible.

"Nancy Wolfe said she could show us those houses tonight if you're not too tired." Dan tugged at the leash to pull the puppy away from the dog food.

Jess had hoped to go over her mother's journal again. There were mountains of reports she'd thought she might go through a second time just in case she missed something before. She'd thought about dropping by the hospital to see if Stinnett was up to an interview. Atmore and Knowles were sticking with their story of a tall man with dark hair having held and tortured them. Those two were being released tomorrow. One way or the other Jess had to get one of them to talk. The news about Campbell's murder hadn't done the job. Maybe Stinnett would talk when she'd had time to think about it.

DEBRA WEBB

On top of all that, they needed to check on Dan Senior and Cook.

"I'll make a deal with you," she offered. "We go by the hospital first, check on your dad and Cook, and see if Stinnett will talk to me, and then we'll make a final decision on a house. *Tonight.*"

"Deal." Dan searched Jess's face. "You still think Stinnett will be the one to break?" The puppy wound around his legs as he spoke.

Jess took the leash from him and unwound the rascal. "I do."

"Mr. Burnett."

They both turned to the tech who'd called Dan's name. The young woman smiled. She was tall and gorgeous with long dark hair. *Spears's type.* Jess banished the thought. As much as she wanted to deny the concept, she doubted she would ever again be able to see a woman with those features without thinking of Spears.

"Dr. Linda is ready for you now," the tech announced.

"Thank you." Dan placed his hand at the small of Jess's back and together they followed the tech.

Jess lifted her chin and kicked Spears out of her head. She was anxious to meet Dr. Linda Hankins. She and Dan had gone to Brighton Academy together. Jess was impressed with how clean and bright the clinic was. Hankins had done a lovely job of making the clinic inviting for people and pets alike.

144

Jess stifled a groan as she considered that she still had to choose a pediatrician for the baby. Apparently, that was something you had to do right away. She didn't understand why she had to do it now. It wasn't like she was going to need one for another seven months. Her OB had said something about the best pediatricians having waiting lists. Tomorrow she would make some calls.

The door opened and an attractive woman breezed into the room. Jess wasn't surprised that Linda was easy on the eyes. All Dan's friends were attractive, especially the women.

"I can't believe I have the famous Daniel Burnett in my clinic," Linda teased.

Dan gave her a hug. "I'm the one who can't believe you made time for us. You're only the most popular veterinarian in the city."

"You always were a charmer."

"Linda, this is Jess Harris, my fiancé."

Linda grinned. "You're the big celebrity who came from Quantico." Linda patted Dan on the shoulder. "You're a lucky guy, Burnett. I can't open a paper or turn on the television without seeing this lady's pretty face."

Jess liked her already. "It's a pleasure to meet you, Linda." Jess offered her hand.

Linda ignored the hand and gave her a bear hug. "Anyone who can have Dan over here wearing that goofy grin is someone I want to know." She laughed. "This must be the one, Dan."

Dan looked at Jess then. "She's definitely the one. She always has been."

While Linda examined the yellow lab and checked for a chip, Dan told Linda about how he and Jess met in high school. Jess couldn't help herself, she laughed so much at their antics as he retold them that her side hurt. She suddenly realized that she couldn't remember ever being this happy, not even when they were teenagers. Life had been too filled with angst, self-doubt, and the need to prove something back then.

No matter where her big dreams had taken her in the past, this was where she was supposed to be. Jess watched Dan as he and Linda chatted. His smile, his every mannerism were indelibly etched on her heart and soul. She thought of her sister and all the years she'd missed spending time with her and her family. Then she thought of her team and she knew without doubt, she would never regret coming home again. She would only regret the nightmare that followed her here.

By the time they said their goodbyes and left Linda's clinic, they not only knew the puppy had no chip, they had named him, gotten his vaccinations, and had the paperwork for officially registering him.

"You want to drop off Bear, go to the hospital, and then grab something to eat before we meet Nancy?"

Jess laughed. Would they ever have a truly free evening? Probably not. "Sounds good to me." Linda had helped pick the name. She'd suggested Bear because the puppy was going to be a very large dog.

A big dog was good. Jess wanted all the protection she could get for their child.

UAB HOSPITAL. 6:50 P.M.

Both Dan Senior and Cook were doing well. Jess was amazed at how chipper Dan's dad appeared. All Cook could talk about was getting back to work. He was so young, Jess wasn't sure he understood how very close he had come to dying.

"Should I wait out here?" Dan asked as they approached Rory Stinnett's room.

A uniformed officer stood on either side of the door. "You're coming in with me." Jess did not want Dan waiting outside. She wasn't about to feed the rumor mill. In her mind and heart, he was still the chief of police. She wanted the officers to see him that way.

"You're the boss."

"Just remember that when we're looking at houses tonight."

Jess showed her badge to the officers on duty. She was pleased when both referred to Dan as chief and appeared nervous in his presence.

Inside, Rory Stinnett's mother sat next to her bed. Her presence would complicate questioning, but Jess knew that asking the woman to step outside would create even more tension.

"Hello, Rory." Jess propped a big smile in place. "I'm sure you remember me. Deputy Chief Harris? This is Chief of Police Burnett. We wanted to check on you and ask you a few questions."

So far Stinnett had said little about her time in captivity and even less about the man who inflicted her wounds, mental as well as physical.

Stinnett's expression was guarded as usual. "I remember you," she said to Jess.

Mrs. Stinnett picked up on her daughter's distress. "I'm not sure it's good for her to be upset just now. Can you come back another time?"

"We'll be brief, Mrs. Stinnett." The excuse was the same every time Jess dropped by. With Knowles and Atmore sticking by their stories of the dark-haired man, Jess needed someone to ID Eric Spears. "Just one question, really."

The women exchanged a look.

Jess opted for another tactic. "Actually, I don't even need to ask a question. I really only need to give Rory something to think about."

The women stared at Jess expectantly.

Jess asked herself again if this was a mistake. The Stinnett family would likely bring in an attorney and complain about Jess, but what she was about to say was the truth. Whether anyone liked it or not, it had to be said.

"Rory, I understand why you're being so careful about what you say to us. You're afraid. Your anxiety is understandable."

If Jess had any doubts whether the woman was holding back, those doubts vanished in the wake of the flash of fear on her face.

"He warned you not to talk," Jess surmised. "He probably said if you told us anything he would be back. I understand you're doing what you believe will keep you and your family safe. I just wanted to let you know I understand."

Something like relief clouded Stinnett's face.

"Chief Burnett and I couldn't come by the hospital without saying hello. We had other patients to visit. An officer investigating this case almost died after he was attacked by one of Spears's followers. And the Chief's father was visited by the man who kidnapped you. I'm just thankful you all survived, that's very rare."

"We're blessed," Stinnett's mother said as she visibly tightened her grip on her daughter's hand.

"Yes, ma'am," Jess agreed. She shook her head then. "Unfortunately, Presley Campbell wasn't so lucky."

Stinnett's face paled. "She's dead?" The words were barely a whisper.

"Yes. Brutally murdered. He slashed her body to pieces, but first he viciously raped her over and over. You can't even imagine." Jess shuddered. "Anyway, I wanted to let you know we're doing all we can to catch him. I don't want you and the others who survived to have to spend the rest of your lives worrying about when he'll come after you again."

Both women's eyes grew large with fear. The mother demanded, "What do you mean?"

Jess shrugged. "Rory is a witness. No matter what he told her, she can identify him. Eric Spears won't forget that. If we can't stop him, he could show up again whenever he pleases." Jess smiled sadly. "We should go. You can call if you need anything or think of something that might help our investigation. Good night, ladies."

The silence in the room was deafening as Jess and Dan exited.

At least now Stinnett fully understood the circumstances.

She would never truly be free as long as Eric Spears was out there.

No one would.

3309 DELL ROAD, MOUNTAIN BROOK, 9:50 P.M.

Nancy Wolfe had to be the most patient woman Jess had ever met. They had gone from house number one to house number two and then three, twice already. Nancy took the whole back and forth between the houses in stride. Thankfully, the homes were only a few streets apart, still it was enough to make a person's head spin. Jess's included.

"Any of the three would be lovely," Nancy reminded them. "I must admit, this one is my favorite."

That was the first time the realtor had confessed to having a favorite. Jess turned to Dan. "I think this one's my favorite, too."

Dan grinned. "I was hoping you'd say that." He looked around the generous great room with its soaring coffered ceilings, deep crown molding, and gorgeous wood floors. "Nancy, if you wouldn't mind, we'll take another walk through."

Nancy waved him off. "Take your time, Dan. I'm at your disposal all night if necessary. I'll just sit on the porch and check my messages."

When the front door closed behind the realtor, Jess walked to the center of the room and turned all the way around. "I can't believe we're thinking of buying this house."

"Four bedrooms, four and a half baths. Every amenity we could possibly want sitting on two acres and only three miles from the academy." Dan joined her and slid his arms around her waist. "If this is the one you want, it's yours."

Jess took a deep breath. "I love you, Dan, with all my heart and I would love nothing better than to have this amazing house as our home." She took a moment to gather her composure. "We can turn that sitting room in the master suite into a nursery." She smiled up at him. "It's perfect."

Rather than say a word, he kissed her so tenderly, so lovingly she couldn't stop the tears. When at last he drew back, he whispered. "I love you, Jess. This is the one."

She smiled and swiped at the blasted tears. "Let's tell Nancy."

Nancy looked up when they stepped out onto the front porch. The soft landscape lighting allowed Jess to see the broad smile that spread across her face as she stood. The lady already knew their answer. "This is the one, isn't it?" she guessed.

Dan extended his hand. "This is the one."

When they'd all shaken hands and hugged to boot, they went inside to sign the papers. The offer was for full asking price. Neither Jess nor Dan wanted to haggle and risk losing this home.

After Nancy drove away, they stood in the driveway and stared at their new home for a while. Perhaps it was premature to consider it theirs, yet it felt like home already.

"I can't wait to show it to Lil." Jess could hardly contain her excitement.

"Nancy is probably calling Mom right now."

They laughed together and Jess took his hands in hers. "You know, there's an amazing sofa on that screened porch around back."

"I was just thinking the same thing."

He scooped her into his arms and carried her to the back porch. By the time he settled her on her feet once more, she was tearing at the buttons of his shirt.

Her cell chimed with an incoming text.

Jess ignored it. She kicked her bag aside and reached for the side closure of her dress. She wanted out of these clothes and in his arms.

That annoying chime sounded again. She groaned.

"You might as well check it," he said as he reached for his belt. "You won't be able to put it out of your mind unless you do."

Jess sighed. "It could be Rory Stinnett. Maybe my not so subtle warning got to her."

"Check the message." Dan sat down and started tugging off his shoes.

Jess dug for her phone. The sooner she got this over with, the sooner she could get back to Dan. Her fingers closed around the phone and she checked the screen. The text message was from...*Tormenter.*

"Shit."

Dan came to her side. He took the phone from her and swiped the screen.

Lovely choice, Jess. I hope Dan has plenty of life insurance.

CHAPTER FOURTEEN

Chet closed the file he'd brought home from work. He was beginning to wonder if the Chief had been right when she'd mentioned the possibility that the reverend had lapsed into dementia toward the end. Henshaw had been leaving messages for sure, presumably for the chief, but the passages gave them a lot of nothing.

Lori sat down on the sofa next to him. "We should hit the sack. I'm beat."

Man, he loved this woman. Even in one of his t-shirts she looked as sexy as hell. She was beautiful and smart and she deserved way better than him. "Me, too."

"You think the investigations on the murders in Scottsboro as well as the reverend's will be closed based on the selfies North sent his sister?"

"I'm guessing all but Amanda will be chalked up to North."

"Jess is certain Spears murdered Amanda."

"I agree." His signature was hard to miss. Harper hoped he got the chance to put one right between that bastard's eyes.

"I wish the photo of Dority would help clear Burnett." Lori sighed and snuggled closer to Chet.

"I know. It sucks. But if North killed her, why change his MO? Why strangle Dority?"

"That's easy," Lori argued. "Spears wanted her murder pinned on Burnett. The MO had to be different. Plus North had to wait for the right opportunity. Burnett's human. Spears knew he'd breakdown and go visit Dority to try and work things out at some point. North had to get in and get out fast. He couldn't afford to stage his victim the way he did the ones in Scottsboro."

"You think North was watching Burnett?"

"Having Burnett under surveillance would explain why Jess and I suddenly stopped seeing him around until just a few days ago. I think he's been tailing Burnett for an opportunity to set him up. He found that chance with Dority."

"Then why take Nina Baron?" Chet countered. "He's got Burnett where he wants him. Why grab Nina? Why not Burnett's third wife, what's her name? You know, Andrea's mother."

"Annette Denton."

"Yeah, Annette. Wouldn't she be easier to manipulate? Why take someone from that clinic? How does he expect to use Nina?"

Lori shook her head. "I don't know. I'm think-ing Nina is some sort of insurance. Jess said some-thing about Nina's meds. If she's off her meds long enough she might have some serious problems. Delusions and paranoia are real worries. Especially if she's being manipulated by someone."

"There has to be some reason he chose her over Annette," Chet argued. "We should ask the chief if something happened while Burnett and Nina were married that maybe caused the divorce or foreshad-owed some event Spears wants to set up."

"Whatever it was," Lori said, "you can bet the Barons kept it quiet."

"Even though we set him back I'm still worried Spears has some sort of big finale coming real soon." Chet's arms tightened around her.

"I don't think that part of his plan has changed."

Chet shook his head. "No, I mean something dif-ferent from the way we figured this would play out. The whole taking six women the way he usually does when he sets a game in motion is out the window. His big finale with the chief being victim six isn't going to happen now."

"Now there's only Nina."

"You can bet he has a plan." Not knowing that plan scared the crap out of Chet and he wasn't easy to scare.

"We know Chester is safe," Lori reminded him.

"But you're not." Chet was worried that Spears would come after Lori. Part of him wanted to tie her up and lock her away some place safe. Then she'd only kick his butt when he let her loose again.

She stroked his jaw with soft, cool fingers. "None of us will be safe until this is over."

"I'm worried," Chet admitted.

"We'll get through this. Spears's plans are falling apart. Look at the risk he took going after Burnett's dad, and the way he appeared to act on pure impulse when he murdered Campbell. He'll make another overt move soon and then maybe he'll make a mistake that will get him caught."

"I want him dead." Chet wasn't going to sugar coat his feelings on the matter. "If I get a shot I'm taking him out."

Lori considered his words for a long moment. "I'm with you. He doesn't deserve to live."

Chet searched her eyes. "We should talk to Corlew. With all three of us working together we should be able to figure out a way to draw him out." His words were barely a whisper. It was crazy but part of him couldn't help feeling that Spears watched and listened to every move and sound they made.

Lori chewed her lip for a moment. "I've considered the possibility myself. We'd need bait."

Bait was the big ass obstacle Chet couldn't see how to get past. "He wants Burnett. Maybe we should talk to him, too. We all worked damned well together on Friday."

"Jess would never forgive us. I couldn't keep something like that from her. I felt like I was betraying her the other day. I can't do that again."

"Even if it meant saving her life?"

Lori leaned her head back on the sofa. "What if we helped Burnett get himself killed? He and Jess are having a baby. Do we really want to be in any way responsible for that kind of tragedy?"

Chet heaved a disgusted breath. "You're right. Just wishful thinking, I guess."

"Do you want to talk about something not so depressing?" Lori grinned up at him.

"Does it include having sex?" He really, really wanted to make love to her. If he was lucky, he'd be making love to Lori every day for the rest of his life.

Lori straddled his lap and wrapped her arms around his neck. "Possibly." She pressed down against him and he groaned.

"Anything you want baby, just name it." He slipped both hands beneath her tee and traced the waistband of her slinky panties.

"We need to set a firm date for the wedding. I was thinking June. That's plenty of time for my mom and sister to help me plan everything. Jess will be back on her feet after having the baby. I want her to be my matron of honor."

"Wow. I guess I need to figure out a best man."

Lori glared at him.

"Yeah, yeah," he recalled they'd talked about this already, "Cook is going to be my best man and Chester will be the ring bearer."

Lori relaxed against him once more. The heat between her thighs was setting him on fire. "My sister will be a bridesmaid, too, so we'll need one more groomsman."

"It won't be Hayes." Chet still wanted to kick that guy's ass even though he'd been behaving himself the past couple of days.

"You could ask Burnett."

Chet made a face. "He's cool and everything, but that would be weird."

"I'm having my mom give me away." Lori looked a little sad at the thought of her father. "Seems right since my dad's not here to do it."

"That's a great idea." He curved his palms over her bottom. She shivered. "Do we have to do it in a church?" He hoped that wasn't going to be an issue. The last church wedding he'd had hadn't ended so well.

"I was thinking of an outdoor wedding. Something not so frilly and complicated."

"We should go that route."

She slid her hands down his chest. He was the one shivering now. When she reached into his sweat pants and wrapped her fingers around him, he groaned. She pulled him free of the waistband and guided him to her. He moved her panties aside just enough to nudge his way into her heat. Man, she was on fire.

Lori pressed down onto him and everything else vanished from his mind.

Whatever else happened he had to keep her safe.

CHAPTER FIFTEEN

CEDAR HILL CEMETERY, MIDNIGHT

Buddy shut off the headlights and the engine of his Charger. Roark had called this meeting and Buddy had no clue why. Normally he wouldn't look a gift horse in the mouth, but this abrupt call made him antsy.

Roark was up to something.

Why the hell wasn't he getting out of his car? The bastard asked for this meeting. What was he waiting for?

Another thirty seconds ticked off before the driver's side door of Roark's vehicle opened. Buddy could hardly make out his form. It was cloudy as hell and the moon wasn't shining through for shit. Roark had insisted on meeting in this damned cemetery where there wasn't the first lamppost. He was up to something for sure.

With his hand on his Beretta, Buddy tensed as his passenger door opened. As soon as Roark was seated and the door was shut, he relaxed. Since the guy didn't have his weapon drawn he wasn't planning to shoot just yet. There was no way he could know that Buddy had been taping their conversations. Buddy hadn't played those tapes for anyone. Not even Jess.

Time to find out. "I haven't slept in two days, Roark. What's this about?"

"You've been playing me." Roark's right hand came around with a .22 leveled on Buddy.

Well, hell. He must have had the damned thing up his sleeve. Probably stolen from the evidence room. He'd shoot Buddy with it and then put it back. Eventually the ballistics would lead to the poor dumb bastard who'd had the .22 in his possession last. It wouldn't be the first time Roark had pulled that kind of stunt.

"What the hell, Roark?"

"Keep both hands on the wheel, Corlew," Roark warned.

Clenching the steering wheel, Buddy went for broke. "I don't know what's got you so pissed off, but it sure as hell doesn't have anything to do with me."

"You've been playing me," Roark repeated.

Buddy stared at him, tried to read his face in the near darkness. Where was the damned moon when he needed it? "What the hell are you talking about?"

"Frank Teller got all the charges against you dropped. How did you get Teller for a lawyer? You like to brag about being this big deal PI, but I know for a fact you don't have that kind of dough, which tells me you had help. Since when have you and Burnett been such good friends?"

DEBRA WEBB

Buddy should have known that would come back to bite him in the ass. "You think I'm stupid, Roark?"

"Well, I don't know. That depends on what you say next. I thought we were friends. I've helped you out when you needed it and you've done the same for me. Now I'm not so sure whose back you're scratching."

Roark had covered for him a couple of times back in the day when Buddy had been on the force. He'd let his drinking get out of control and showed up for work inebriated. Roark had even taken care of a few missing reports Buddy had failed to submit during those bad years. But there had always been an ulterior motive, Buddy just hadn't known it until Roark started his anti-Burnett campaign. Roark could pretend they were friends, but it couldn't be further from the truth.

"Look, Burnett put Teller on my case without asking me. Then he comes around slapping me on the back like we've been friends forever." Buddy grunted. "Yeah, right."

"Then why'd he send his lawyer over to help you out?"

"He wants me to try and lure Spears out." Buddy laughed. "Dumbass thinks just because I got some inside info from that crazy Amanda Brownfield that I can get Spears's attention. He's desperate to protect Jess."

Roark laughed until he lost his breath. "You mean Burnett hasn't figured out yet that you're the

162

last person he should be asking to help Jess? Doesn't he know you want her for yourself?"

Buddy struggled with the anger that lit inside him. "Doesn't matter now, does it? They found that pic of Dority with that Spears's follower. Burnett'll be cleared."

"Don't be so quick to jump to conclusions. The mother's testimony is solid. As of right now, if you ask me, Burnett is still suspect number one. It'll be official soon enough."

Buddy turned toward Roark and pumped as much worry into his tone as he could dredge up. "If we need to do something else to ensure the case against him is airtight, just tell me. I'm your man."

"Burnett is going down, Corlew. End of story. Whether he's charged with murder or not his career in law enforcement is over. And I'm finally getting that promotion. I need to get my time in as captain before I retire."

Buddy faked a laugh. "You're not that old, man. What's the hurry?"

Roark shook his head. "Damned diabetes, high blood pressure. It just keeps piling up. The next thing I know they'll be forcing me to retire. I want to retire with my time in as a captain, by God. I deserve it."

"The health stuff sucks, but that's good news about the promotion." Buddy needed the guy to spit out whatever it was he knew about Burnett. He was ready to be done with this a-hole. "I still say that photo will clear Burnett."

DEBRA WEBB

"You ever watch that old Hitchcock movie *Rear Window*?"

"Course." Buddy wasn't actually sure but it sounded familiar.

"There's just one thing that could clear Burnett of Dority's murder and no one is ever going to know. Trust me on that."

"Whatever you say, Roark. Hey, maybe you can tell Black to cut me some slack from now on. He's always busting my balls."

"You keep me informed on what you hear from Burnett or his woman and I'll keep our new chief of police off your back."

"I can do that," Buddy assured him.

Roark got out and walked back to his car. The man should have retired long ago in Buddy's opinion. But then again the job was all he had. His wife had left him years ago. She'd turned his kids against him, to hear Roark tell it. Being a cop was all that mattered to him. The idea made Buddy feel a little bad about what he was doing. He shook it off. Roark had made his own bed. Buddy couldn't let him destroy Dan. Jess would never forgive him if he did.

Sometimes it was hard being such a nice guy.

When Roark had driven away Buddy shut off the hidden recorder. He googled *Rear Window* and read the synopsis of the movie.

"Well, well." Buddy shook his head at the idea of what the guy had done. The bastard had some balls, he'd give him that. "Gotcha, Roark."

CHAPTER SIXTEEN

"We're ready to proceed when you are, Lieutenant Colbert," Frank Teller announced.

Dan had dropped by the hospital to check on his dad first thing this morning. The doctors had agreed that he could go home tomorrow. His dad couldn't wait. After that, Dan had gone by Nancy Wolfe's office to sign a few more documents. She would set up the closing as soon as possible. Though no financing was necessary, there were still steps that had to be taken. Purchasing the house outright required using a serious portion of his trust fund, but having no mortgage on the property guaranteed Jess didn't have to worry. The seller had only been too happy to accept their offer. As soon as this meeting was concluded he intended to take care of the vehicle purchases. He hoped Jess would have time at some point today to try out a couple of options. Then there was furniture shopping—

"Let's begin." Anne Colbert took a seat at the conference table and arranged her notes. "This proceeding is being recorded so please identify yourselves."

Dan resisted the urge to shake his head. "Chief of Police Daniel Burnett."

"Franklin Teller, counsel for Chief of Police Burnett."

"As you know," Colbert began, "this is an Internal Affairs investigation to determine whether you, Chief Burnett, have violated any department policies with respect to your conduct in the Captain Ted Allen and Meredith Dority cases. This is not a criminal proceeding. If the department believes that it has sufficient evidence against you it will be for the DA's Office to determine how to proceed."

For the next half hour, Colbert questioned Dan about the timeframe around Captain Ted Allen's disappearance.

"I understand that you believe, then," Colbert said, "that someone planted Allen's cell phone and wedding band on or near your property?"

"Yes," Dan answered. "Both items were discovered in areas easily accessed by the public. In fact, the phone was found on the street amid garbage that had spilled from my trashcan. The ring was in the barbecue grill that sat on my rear patio."

"You will note," Frank added, "that around that same time frame, Chief Burnett's home was broken into and recording devices planted. Clearly, someone had trespassed on his property and carried out a number of criminal activities."

"Please, Mr. Teller, refrain from making comments unless you have an objection. Chief Burnett is capable of responding to my questions."

"Yes, Lieutenant."

"Chief Burnett, have you at any time during the Allen investigation, attempted to or impeded the investigation that included evidence potentially detrimental to you?"

"No, I have not."

"Have you cooperated in the Allen investigation with respect to evidence that could be detrimental to you?"

"Yes, I have."

"Have you, at any time during the investigation, ordered anyone in the department to compromise the investigation in any way such as by the destruction of evidence?"

"No, I have not." Dan held his mounting fury in check. As necessary as he knew this proceeding to be the entire ordeal felt absurd.

"Did your belief that Captain Allen had tried to kill Deputy Chief Jess Harris cause you to treat the investigation into Captain Allen's disappearance differently than you would have otherwise?"

"Definitely not."

Colbert turned to the next page in her many notes. "The one concern I have is the complaint Captain Allen purportedly intended to file against you."

"That complaint was never filed," Frank argued.

"Clearly," Colbert replied dryly.

"From the beginning," Dan offered, "I acknowledged the friction between Captain Allen and Deputy Chief Harris and worked in my capacity as chief of police to correct the issue. Captain Allen was not happy with my reprimand for his disrespect to a fellow division chief who is also his superior. I believe the unfiled report was his way of responding."

Colbert wrote more notes on her pad. "Moving on to your involvement in the Meredith Dority case. Given the allegations against you by Ms. Dority and your relationship with her, am I correct that you have had no role in the investigation, other than to respond to the department's questions?"

Dan braced for tougher questions. This part of his troubles was far more complicated. "Yes, that's correct."

"You were married for a brief time approximately nineteen years ago?"

"Yes."

"Did the marriage end under amicable circumstances?"

"Yes. In fact we continued to work together for several years after the divorce."

"You've stated previously that you have no idea why she decided to assert allegations against you related to your work as liaison between the mayor's office and the Birmingham Police Department, is that correct?"

"Yes. The news was a total shock to me and all who know me."

Frank passed a manila envelope across the table. "You'll find more than a dozen character witness statements in this file. Most of the witnesses worked with Chief Burnett during the time in question."

Colbert accepted the file and placed it with the others. "Thank you, Mr. Teller. I reserve the right to question any and all witnesses."

"Of course," Frank agreed.

"On the morning of Ms. Dority's murder," Colbert began, "you visited her. Was this in your capacity as chief of police?"

"No." Dan wished a thousand times he could take back his actions that day. Not only would he have held onto his temper, he would have insisted on staying longer and checking on her mother. Maybe Meredith would still be alive if he'd been concerned with her motives rather than his own.

"During your visit you argued about her accusations against you, is that correct?"

"Yes." Dan had recounted the events of that morning numerous times. He was telling the truth. No amount of questioning was going to change his story.

"You must have realized that the department might have to investigate her claims at some point. Would you agree the visit was most imprudent, Chief?"

"Yes. I see that now."

Frank's cell vibrated against the table. He snatched it up and made a face at whatever he found on the screen. "I apologize, but I need a moment to take this."

Colbert shot him a look over the top of her reading glasses. "Make it quick, Mr. Teller. Our time is as valuable as yours."

Frank nodded and stepped into the corridor.

Dan worked at staying relaxed. "How are you adjusting to the Alabama heat, Lieutenant?"

Colbert rolled her eyes. "Don't ask. It's insufferable."

Dan laughed in spite of himself. "It surely can be." He wanted to ask what brought her south, but opted not to. He rubbed at the tension in his neck. He would be damned glad when this was over.

"I have an aunt here," she said as if she'd read his mind. "The last of my mother's side of the family. She's not doing so well these days. I didn't want her to spend her final years without family around her."

"I'm certain she appreciates you being here."

Colbert smiled for the first time. "Most days."

The door opened and Frank walked in, right behind him was Buddy Corlew and Harold Black.

Before Dan could ask what was going on, Colbert demanded, "What is the meaning of this, Mr. Teller?"

"Lieutenant Colbert, we have new evidence to present," Frank announced.

Dan looked from Frank to the others. Corlew grinned and Harold looked grim.

"This is highly irregular, Mr. Teller. It had better be good," Colbert warned, rising to her feet.

"Gentlemen, please identify yourselves for the record."

"Harold Black, Acting Chief of Police." Harold glanced at Dan, a sadness in his expression.

Dan hadn't found an opportunity to tell him how deeply sorry he was to hear about his wife. The somber news made all this seem damned petty.

"Buddy Corlew, private detective," Corlew spoke up next.

"So, what is this about, Chief Black," Colbert asked.

"Lieutenant, Mr. Corlew has found evidence that proves Chief Burnett couldn't possibly have been involved with the murder of Meredith Dority."

"Why don't we all have a seat and review this evidence?" Colbert suggested.

The next few minutes were a whirlwind of conversations recorded by Corlew. Dan couldn't believe what he was hearing.

"I have the witness's signed statement right here." Harold passed a copy to Colbert. "I visited him personally just an hour ago."

The IA investigator read over the document. "You're telling me that this witness provided a statement to Lieutenant Roark days ago that cleared Chief Burnett?"

"That's correct," Harold confirmed.

"You may summarize the statement aloud, Chief Black," Colbert directed.

"Mr. Alfred Zacharias lives in the home directly across the street from Meredith Dority's mother,"

Black began. "Due to his physical disabilities he is homebound. He considers himself a sort of neighborhood watchman. From his living room window, Mr. Zacharias watched the exchange between Chief Burnett and Meredith Dority through her open front door. Four or five minutes after Chief Burnett departed, Mr. Zacharias saw another man knock on Dority's door. This man was tall with dark hair and he wore sunglasses. He drove a black Infiniti with an obscured license plate. Meredith Dority answered the door and the man went inside. The door closed behind him. Five or so minutes later the man left. The man Mr. Zacharias described fits that of the now deceased suspect, Quentin North, who owned a black Infiniti at the time. We've also learned that Mr. North took a photo of himself with Dority and sent it to his sister on the same day Dority was murdered. Mr. Zacharias stated that he gave this same statement to Lieutenant Roark that very afternoon."

Stunned wasn't an adequate description of what Dan felt at the moment.

"Where is Lieutenant Roark?" Colbert demanded.

"We issued a warrant for his arrest." Harold stood. "If you have no further questions, I'm planning to make the arrest personally."

"You may go, Chief Black," Colbert said.

Harold gave a nod and left without looking at Dan. Roark had been Harold's right hand for more than a decade. This was a devastating blow.

"Lieutenant," Frank said, "the IAB should find no misconduct by Chief Burnett and permit him to resume his duties immediately. Clearly, there are persons working to discredit him. Chief Burnett's outstanding record speaks for itself."

Colbert took a moment to consider Frank's request. "I will need time to review the evidence. There are still a number of outstanding questions. Although, it appears that Chief Burnett's conduct comports with the department's protocol with respect to the Dority and Allen cases, which is the only concern of the IAB, I must complete the investigation. I'll advise you of the IAB's findings as soon as possible."

"Thank you, Lieutenant Colbert."

When Colbert had left the conference room, Frank shook first Dan's hand and then Corlew's. "You'll be back in office before the week is out, Dan."

"I can live with that timeline."

Frank grabbed his briefcase. "I have to get back to the office. Thank you again, Mr. Corlew."

After Frank was out the door, Dan closed it. "How did you get Roark to come clean?"

Corlew held up his hands. "That's a trade secret, Danny boy." He shrugged. "Besides, I owed you one."

Jess had told Dan last week that she'd asked Corlew to look into who in the department was trying to discredit him. Dan hadn't been too happy about it at the time. It looked as if he'd misjudged Corlew. Maybe the man had changed.

DEBRA WEBB

"Whatever the case, thank you." Dan thrust out his hand.

Corlew shook it. "No big deal."

"Right." Dan picked up his briefcase. "What about that other matter I discussed with you."

"Are you sure you want to go down that path?"

"What I don't want to do is waste any more time. Make the call, Corlew." Dan wanted this over for Jess and for him.

"And if you get yourself killed, how am I supposed to explain it to Jess?"

Dan took a second to get his temper under control. "If you won't do it for me, do it for her. I'm willing to take the risk if it means a chance at keeping Spears away from her."

"You're just assuming Spears would give me the time of day. I'm pretty sure he knows I'm the one who got his location through Amanda."

"Good. Then maybe he'll respond just to get a shot at both of us."

CHAPTER SEVENTEEN

Lieutenant Kelvin Roark lived in a split-level ranch style home in a quiet neighborhood in Pelham that reminded Jess of the Brady Bunch house. The only things missing were the wife and the kids.

"How much longer before SWAT is in place?" she asked, adjusting her bulletproof vest.

Roark had been tipped off about his impending arrest and evidently suffered a meltdown. He'd threatened to blow up his house if anyone else dared to enter. Houses within a four-block radius had been evacuated.

Under the circumstances, Jess understood standing back even if she hated, hated, hated waiting. Especially when the man inside the house was responsible for so much of Dan's pain. The very idea that he'd known from day one that Dan couldn't possibly have murdered Meredith Dority made Jess want to barge in there and bust his kneecaps before he was arrested.

"Five minutes." Harold Black's voice was as somber as his expression as he, too, readied to forcibly enter the home of the cop who'd been his friend and right hand for more than a decade.

"I appreciate your team taking care of this situation," Black said, as if reading her thoughts. "I didn't want the men and women he'd worked alongside to be the ones to do this. I'd like to keep what we have to do as respectful as possible. After all, he is one of us."

"It might have been nice if he'd showed some of that respect for Dan." There was a lot more Jess could say, but she left it at that.

According to the briefing, Roark had been working for weeks, maybe months, to make Dan look bad. He'd held it against Dan for making chief of police instead of Black four years ago. Roark had been waiting for the right opportunity to render a little payback and maybe to see that his friend got the promotion Roark believed he deserved. From what Jess had heard, the man had a history of playing dirty behind the scenes. How had Black managed to ignore his deceit for so long? Giving Black grace, sometimes people saw what they wanted to see. It made life a lot less complicated.

"If it's any consolation," Black offered, "I knew Dan was innocent, and I was doing all within my power to clear up this unholy mess."

Jess didn't doubt Black's sincerity on the matter. "Let's just get this done."

Harper and Hayes were holding positions in the tree line on the back of the property. Lori would move in from the front along with Jess and Black once SWAT had done its part. Whether Roark actually had a bomb in his possession or not, he was certainly armed. Thankfully, no one else was in the home. Roark's wife had left him long ago. His two adult children were estranged from him and living out of state. The part that worried Jess the most was the comments he'd made about his health to Corlew. Even a man as seemingly heartless as Roark, had a breaking point.

Glass shattered, signaling the use of the flash-bang grenade to disorient and subdue the suspect.

"Here we go," Black said as the battering ram splintered Roark's front door.

The adrenaline firing through Jess had her ready to move. A loud pop warned someone had discharged a weapon.

"Shots fired!" echoed across the communication links.

"Lord have mercy," Black murmured.

"Clear!" seared in Jess's brain via the earpiece she wore.

"Move in," she directed her team.

The rush across the neatly mown grass and up the steps was quiet. The lack of talk in the house worried Jess. The team commander waited in the living room.

"Lieutenant Roark is dead," he said quietly. "He's in the bedroom. Second door on the left upstairs. He fired one shot into his brain with his service weapon."

Black heaved a heavy breath. "Someone call the coroner."

Lori was on her cell before Black finished the statement.

Jess followed Black up the short flight of stairs and down the hall to Roark's bedroom. Roark sat in a chair next to the bed, his head dropped back, the missing upper portion splattered across the wall behind him. He'd placed photos of his former wife and children on the table next to him.

Black sighed again, tears dampening his cheeks. "Sweet Jesus." He shook his head.

Jess put a hand on his arm. "Chief, maybe you should go on back to the office and let us take care of this."

He nodded. "I think that might be wise."

When he turned away from his old friend, Jess flinched at the devastation on his face. She was forty-two years old and for most of that time she'd never considered herself a hugger. Public displays of emotion weren't a part of her way of doing things, particularly with someone she considered more enemy than friend. Since coming back home to Birmingham, she'd found herself hugging more than she had in all the years of her adult life combined.

Still, she hugged Harold Black. He needed a hug and she was there. Black's shoulders shook with the pain he felt. When he'd regained his composure,

Jess gave him a sad smile. "I'll keep you posted on things here."

Black nodded and went on his way.

"Crime scene van is en route," Lori announced as she entered the room.

"Let's go through the steps. Make sure he didn't leave a note or any other evidence we might need."

"On it."

Jess turned back to the man who had served the Birmingham Police Department for so many years whether always on the straight and narrow or not. Power was a dangerous impetus. His motive for crossing the line between good and evil, no matter how he rationalized it, had cost him everything.

Today was a bittersweet triumph. Dan had been cleared of any suspicion in Dority's murder, but a cop had lost his battle with the dark side.

Jess owed Buddy. He'd really come through for Dan. She hoped the two of them would finally put their past rivalries behind them.

Her cell clanged and Jess dug it from her bag. *Gant calling.*

She hoped they had unearthed a lead to Spears. "You have something new?" Jess asked as she moved around Roark's bedroom checking for evidence of any other wrongdoing the man had been stirring up.

"We're at the Argyle Drive house," Gant said, sounding as if he were in a hole. "We found Spears's escape route."

Jess was glad to hear it. She still shuddered whenever she thought about the text Spears had sent while they were standing on the back porch at their new house. She wanted that house to be a new beginning with no lingering ghosts related to Spears. She wanted the new life she and Dan had begun free of the SOB.

"Did you find any evidence that might tell us where he went from there?" He'd escaped, that was clear. What they needed was a trail to follow. Dammit, he couldn't keep getting away clean.

"What we found is a message. To *you.*"

As much as the news unnerved her, it wasn't news at all. Spears loved taunting her with his messages.

"I'm on my way."

669 ARGYLE DRIVE. BIRMINGHAM. 4:30 P.M.

Lori parked her Mustang in front of the big house. "You okay?"

Jess nodded. "Sure." She had Roark's blood on her new turquoise pencil skirt, and she was damned tired.

"I know we're not where we'd like to be on this investigation, but some things took a turn in the right direction today, Jess," Lori assured her, stepping out of detective mode. She never referred to Jess by her first name on the job.

Jess wrestled up a smile. "Dan was cleared of Dority's murder. That's a tremendous relief."

"Spears is getting more and more erratic which means he's bound to make a mistake that will help us," Lori went on. "If he's intent on seeing this through, his options are narrowing. It seems to me there's a good chance this will be over sooner rather than later."

"True," Jess allowed. "If he was half as smart as he thought he was, he'd have taken off by now."

For some reason Jess couldn't hold back a laugh, and once she started she couldn't stop. Maybe it was the idea that they were sitting in front of the house Spears had used for months without anyone knowing. Or, perhaps it was the fact that he had murdered so many people right here in Birmingham and they were no closer to catching him today than they had been two months ago. Lori joined her. If anyone was watching or was close enough to hear, they would surely think she and Lori had gone around the bend.

Jess fell silent. She turned to her friend. "I'm terrified." She hadn't said those words out loud to anyone, not even to Dan.

Lori reached across the console and took her hand. "Me, too."

"Eric Spears spent five years—at least—following a specific pattern down to the letter. Even after he deviated from that pattern and started his new game here, every step was precisely calculated and executed." Jess thought of his most recent crime scenes. "What he did to North and to Campbell was abrupt and frenzied. His kills have always been executed with cold, brutal detachment, never with this hot, uncontrolled emotion."

"You think he's really losing it?" Lori asked quietly. "Like over-the-edge, crazy-as-hell losing it?"

"I think so." Jess blinked at the burn in her eyes. "I'm scared to death every time I say goodbye to Dan that it'll be the last time."

"I know." Lori closed her eyes for a moment. "We've been worried about Chester. What if Spears figures out where he is? What if he kills Chet? What the hell would I do without him and that little boy?"

Jess smiled sadly. "Funny thing is, about two months ago we would've both sworn we weren't interested in permanent relationships, much less children."

Lori laughed. "Can you believe it? You're pregnant and I'm biting my nails with worry about Chet's vasectomy reversal."

A frown tugged at Jess's brow. "Isn't he scheduled for surgery soon?"

"He cancelled until this is over. He didn't want to be out of commission with Spears still out there."

"I can understand his reasoning," Jess squeezed Lori's hand, "but as soon as Spears is out of the way, he should get the surgery." She made a face. "This baby isn't going to have any friends his age if some of my friends don't start procreating."

"Believe me, as soon as things are back in working order, we're going for it."

"Good."

"So you think this baby is going to be a boy?" Lori inquired with a look that suggested she thought Jess might be keeping something from her.

"It's too early to know. Besides, I don't care if it's a boy or a girl. Either one will be great."

"I want a girl since Chet already has a son."

"Nothing wrong with two sons."

"I guess not."

Silence settled around them. Jess stared at the official vehicles lining the street in front of the house. Gant was in there waiting for her. Spears was out there somewhere doing the same thing.

"I believe he's even more dangerous now." The words seemed too loud after the moment of quiet. "The very idea that he hasn't left Birmingham already tells me he's lost any ability to reason. Otherwise, he wouldn't continue to place himself at such risk." In Jess's opinion, that was the bottom line.

"I don't know which one scares me the most," Lori admitted, "the prospect that he's gone totally crazy or the notion that he might just up and disappear."

"I was thinking we should preempt his next move." Jess hoped Lori would see the potential in her plan rather than the risk.

"How are we supposed to know what his next move is? His MO is all over the place now."

Jess inhaled a deep breath and took the plunge. "Instead of waiting helplessly, we make the next move. We lure him in, and then we take him down."

"What does Burnett say about your plan?"

Jess cut her a look. "He doesn't know and I want it to stay that way. Before he's finished, Spears will try to kill him, Lori. I can't let that happen. We've wasted too much time already being reactive rather than proactive."

"We weren't exactly in a position to be anything other than reactive until now. What else could we have done?"

"I know. I know." Jess held up her hands in surrender. "That's my frustration talking. But things are different now. Spears's desperation is showing."

"His pride is driving him," Lori suggested. "He can't lose. Or..."

"Or?" Jess held her breath.

"He can't bear the thought of *not* having you. Like you said, the old Eric Spears would disappear, regroup, and appear again when you least expected him. But he can't do that now. He's grown so obsessed with you, he's lost all semblance of control."

Lori was right. Eric Spears was a torturer-murderer. He and his kind sat at the very top of the evil scale. As complicated and layered as his evil psyche was, what drove him boiled down to a single basic element: *obsession.* Evil began and ended with obsession.

"Whatever he has in mind," Jess agreed, "he needs a way out of the corner he's in while still looking brilliant. His loyal followers have obviously dwindled so he may be on his own at this point."

"When you say *lure* him in," Lori ventured, "what do you have in mind?"

A rap on the car window made them both jump.

Gant stood outside the car. "You coming or what?"

"We'll talk about this later," Jess suggested as she reached for her seatbelt. She emerged from the car and gave Gant a pointed look. "Let's see what you found."

Jess focused on steadying her nerves as they went inside. She didn't have to look as they passed the parlor to know the painting was gone. Dan had made sure it was removed and logged into evidence ASAP.

In the basement turned torture room the walls had been taken apart. Behind a built-in refrigerator was a door. The opening was lower than a typical door and slightly narrower.

"It's an escape tunnel in case the house collapses during a storm. This way the residents wouldn't be trapped under all the rubble," Gant explained.

"Clever. Have you been in there?"

He nodded. "I have. You walk about fifty feet and there's a ladder up to the farthest boundary of the backyard. The exit above ground's well concealed by shrubs and trees."

Jess stepped into the tunnel. Gant followed her. He flipped a switch and light filled the close space. The walls, floors, and ceiling were concrete.

"The message is next to the ladder."

Jess walked to the ladder that provided an egress to the yard above and stared at the words scrawled in a felt-tip marker.

The rules have changed. You won't know who or what to trust, not even yourself.

CHAPTER EIGHTEEN

Three cups of coffee and Buddy still felt like hell. He'd celebrated a little too much last night. The blonde who'd still been in his bed when he woke up this morning reminded him why he never drank himself into oblivion anymore—last night being a major breach of that policy. He ended up in bed with strangers. He did dumb shit like pick fights, which might explain the shiner he was sporting today.

He glanced at his reflection the rearview mirror. "Idiot."

If he was smart he'd go home, crawl back into bed, and sleep about three days. The last five days had been crazy as hell. He'd seen Spears with his own two eyes. Most had doubted him at first, but then yesterday Gant had found the escape route Spears used. Even better, Spears had left a note. Jess let him know last night that Gant and his uptight pals all had to acknowledge that Buddy had been right.

186

Spears was the one doing the reacting now, by God.

"Bastard."

Buddy shifted his attention to the bookstore sitting on the corner. He'd gotten a call from DeeAnn Garner about an hour ago. A book he'd ordered was in. He grunted a laugh. He hadn't read a book since his freshman year in high school. What did he need with fiction? His life could be a thriller by one of those big shot writers. A bestseller.

The book you ordered is in.

The line was a code phrase. DeeAnn had a little extra revenue coming in by acting as a go between. Guys like Buddy, who didn't want anyone who might be watching to know his contacts, used The Book Shop to order a book. DeeAnn handled the rest. If he wanted to get a message to somebody, like Roark, for example—poor bastard—he used The Book Shop. No calls, texts, or emails to trace.

Buddy climbed out of his Charger and ambled to the entrance. The shop was carved out of the corner of an old apartment building only steps from his favorite hangout, The Garage Café.

Maybe after this he'd grab a sandwich and a beer. Anything to ease the throbbing in his skull.

"Idiot," he grumbled again.

Just because Dan Burnett owed him big time and Harold Black actually apologized for treating him like crap—well, he hadn't said the last part but Buddy knew what he meant—was no reason to celebrate with too much Tequila.

Damn if he lived through this day it would be a miracle.

He pushed through the door and bells jingled overhead. Buddy groaned.

"You don't look so good this morning, Buddy."

DeeAnn Garner was a nice lady. She went to church every Sunday and always said please and thank you. She kept that good looking frame of hers wrapped up like a prim little librarian and those pretty eyes hidden behind big glasses. And she was a blonde, Buddy had always had a thing for blondes.

Somewhere under all those modest layers, there was a big secret and one of these days Buddy was going to be the man to peel all those layers back.

But not today.

He pulled off a smile. "I feel a lot worse than I look," he confessed.

"You need to borrow a little concealer for that black eye?" Her lips quirked with the need to smile.

"No, ma'am. It gives me a kind of bad boy charm, don't you think?"

DeeAnn laughed, the sound soft and tinkling. "No one would ever see you as anything else."

Not sure if that was a compliment or not, Buddy moved on. "I'm here to pick up that book I ordered."

"It came just this morning." DeeAnn reached beneath the counter and pulled out a copy of Catch-22. "Interesting choice."

"Maybe my inner reader is trying to tell me something. Thanks." He opted not to tell her that the only 22 he'd seen lately was the business end of the one Roark had been showing off. He tossed forty bucks on the counter and gave her a little salute. "See you next time I hear about a book I just have to read."

DeeAnn shook her head and waved him off.

Buddy hustled back to his Charger and dropped behind the wheel. He skimmed through the pages until he found a small sealed envelope. As usual, there was no name on the front, only a number, #10. Buddy was #10. That meant there were at least nine others who received messages like this. Or maybe the numbers were chosen at random. Whatever.

He tore open the envelope and there was a single typed sentence and no signature.

Meet me at the Garage at two.

Wouldn't be the first time he'd taken a meeting with a stranger.

His gut clenched at the idea that Spears may have sent the message. He had the number Dan had given him…he could text the guy.

No. That would be a mistake. He wasn't about to set in motion a domino effect he couldn't stop. Danny boy's big plan to bait and trap Spears could seriously backfire. Buddy had to spend some sober time thinking it through before he opened that Pandora's box.

Going home and prepping for the meeting was the smart thing to do.

Buddy intended to be a whole lot smarter today than he'd been last night

THE GARAGE CAFÉ. 2:00 P.M.

Buddy settled on a stool at the end of the bar. He was a regular here. The bartender, Casey, would ensure no one bothered him. When he'd entered he'd counted five or six patrons, mostly regulars. Two he didn't recognize.

Black had agreed to keep Buddy's name out of the investigation into Roark's activities. The guy was dead, it wasn't as if they were going to be pressing charges against him. Fear wasn't his reason for wanting his name kept out of the official reports. He was a PI, he depended on input from his sources. He couldn't afford for word to get out that he'd rescued the chief of police by exposing one of his sources.

Not good for business.

He felt bad about Roark, but the guy had made his own choice. Buddy couldn't let him destroy Dan the way he'd destroyed Harper's partner all those years ago. Buddy had done the right thing this time.

In his peripheral vision Buddy watched a man approach. The guy was tall with a distinguished bearing—scratch that, an arrogant bearing. Gray hair and a high-end silk suit.

Damn. A fed.

Buddy downed the remainder of his beer as the suit slid onto the stool beside him.

"It appears you've found yourself in a bit of a Catch-22 situation, Mr. Corlew."

Buddy sat his empty bottle aside and eyed his guest. "Oh yeah? Who says so?"

The man smiled. "My name is John Kurtze, Mr. Corlew. Unfortunately for me, my superior *says* so."

Buddy raised his hand and motioned for Casey to bring another round of the same.

With business slow this time of day, Casey tossed aside the polishing cloth he'd been using on the bar and headed toward Buddy with two sweating long neck bottles of Corona.

"Sparkling water for me, please," Kurtze insisted.

"You can leave both those right here." Buddy nodded to Casey.

Casey left the Coronas and rounded up a bottle of sparkling water for Kurtze. When the bartender was out of earshot, Buddy said, "Why don't you tell me what this is about?"

Kurtze sipped his water before giving Buddy an answer. "I'm afraid I'm not at liberty to share very much with you, Mr. Corlew."

"Why don't you tell me what you are at liberty to share and we can both get on with our lives." Buddy had stuff to do.

"I'm the personal assistant to retired FBI Director Winston Drummond."

"The name doesn't ring a bell." Buddy had never heard of him.

"He's been retired for more than two decades. I'm certain you haven't."

"Does he need a private investigator?" Buddy reached for his beer.

"What he *needs*," Kurtze said emphatically, "is for you to stop digging around in the past."

Since the only past Buddy was currently digging into was Jess's, it wasn't necessary to ask for clarification.

"I was retained to learn the truth about Lee Harris." Buddy swallowed a slug of Corona. "I've never let a client down before and I don't intend to start now."

"Chief Harris will have her answers in time." Kurtze stood and placed a twenty on the counter. "For now, I would strongly encourage you to leave the subject be. Good day, Mr. Corlew."

"Same to you, Mr. Kurtze."

Buddy watched the man go. He hitched his head toward the door and the bartender nodded before disappearing through the kitchen. Buddy savored another long drink of his beer. Twenty or so seconds passed and Casey returned.

"Black Cadillac," Casey reported. "Rental."

"Hmm." Definitely not traveling on the Government's nickel. "Thanks, Casey."

Whatever Jess's father had gotten himself into, it seemed some folks wanted it to stay dead and buried.

CHAPTER NINETEEN

Dan Burnett was no longer a person of interest in Meredith Dority's murder.

Fury ignited inside Eric. He braced his hands against the wall and fought to repress his screams. North had failed him miserably…they had all failed him at this most crucial juncture. If only he had known that insignificant whore had been disloyal to him, he would have made her suffer so much more before putting her out of her misery. Months of preparation, weeks of orchestrating every facet of the perfect plan—all of it was obliterated.

"Is there anything I can do, Eric?"

He whirled around. "Get out of my sight." The only thing he wanted to do right now was to tear someone apart. The need to hear the harrowing screams and to feel the heat of a victim's blood in his hands was a living, pulsing thing.

"It's almost time," the hapless troll dared to remind him. "I've attended to the other, just as you asked."

"I know perfectly well what time it is. Now get out."

Eric closed his eyes and drew in a deep breath. This next step could very well be his last opportunity to wield the agony he so wanted Burnett to feel. He wanted Jess to cry out in anguish. The thought made him so hard he couldn't help touching himself.

There could be no mistakes. He would have this moment.

He turned to the backup plan he'd been keeping to himself for days now. He wouldn't have known about her and that breakdown all those years ago had the troll in the other room not discovered the dirty little secret. Perhaps he had proven his worth after all. His loyalty had thus far been unwavering. Since Quentin's unfortunate lapse in judgment, the troll had been keeping a close eye on Jess. He'd kept Eric well informed of her movements when she wasn't playing deputy chief.

Of all the ruthless killers Eric had commissioned, wasn't it poetic justice that the only truly loyal one turned out to be the least likely candidate?

Finding an employee on vacation from the facility where Nina Baron resided had been as simple as a few clicks on the keyboard. After all, Eric had made his fortune in software security. Nurse Edna Bruhn had taken two weeks off to go visit an old friend in Florida. Sadly, she never left home and since she had no children or husband, no one had noticed. When she didn't report back to work next week, someone would finally wonder what had become of the sixty-six year old. Too bad she hadn't retired in the spring since her personnel file noted her eligibility.

Too, too bad.

Eric summoned a smile. "Now. Let's start again, Nina."

Nina Baron lifted her face and stared at him, terror and disorientation rampant in her dark eyes, quaking through her slim body. Her brown hair fell around her beautiful face, making her look so innocent while the mental illness that no amount of money could evict churned her mind with delusions and paranoia.

Eric leaned down and placed his hands on the arms of her chair. "What did he do to you, Nina?"

She moistened those lovely, pouty lips. "He left me."

"That's right, Nina," Eric placated. Today was the first time she had given the correct response the first time. He had broken her. After nearly a week of fighting him, she had surrendered to him and to her own voices. "Dan deserted you when you needed him most because he wanted *her*."

The shaking worsened. "Where's Dan?"

"I'll take you to him," Eric promised. "You must remember what I expect you to do. You must stop him from hurting your family, Nina."

She wagged her head side to side. "He won't hurt my family." Her mouth worked for a bit before she managed to say the rest. "Dan wouldn't do that."

"He will," Eric roared.

She jumped, and then nodded adamantly. "He will," she repeated, looking anywhere but at Eric. "I'll stop him."

"Everyone is depending on you, Nina. You must stop him. Do you understand?"

She nodded, the movement jerky now.

"Very good, Nina. Now, tell me what you're going to do when I take you to Dan?"

She thought for a moment before she dared to lift her gaze once more. She blinked rapidly as if it hurt to look directly at him.

"What will you do, Nina?" he demanded.

"I'm going to kill him."

CHAPTER TWENTY

The home of Edna Bruhn was a modest cottage. Newspapers had piled up outside and her mail was overflowing from the box at the end of her sidewalk. Her closest neighbor had insisted that Edna had flown down to Tampa, Florida, to spend time with her best friend from high school. Edna was an RN at the clinic where Nina Baron had resided for more than ten years.

But Edna had never made it to Florida. She'd never even made it to the airport. The clinic's administrator, Forrest Desmond, had received a phone call from Edna's friend in Tampa. The friend was worried about her. Edna had left a message last Wednesday saying she wouldn't be able to come to Florida after all. The friend hadn't been able to reach her since. No one was more surprised to hear this news than Desmond. He'd been so concerned that he'd driven right over. Edna hadn't answered the door when he knocked. With her newspapers and mail all piled up he'd decided to call the BPD.

Lieutenant Hayes had kicked the door open and the smell of death had wafted out to greet them. The administrator was currently on the front lawn heaving his guts out.

Lieutenant Hayes passed a handkerchief to Jess.

Holding her breath, she managed to say, "Thank you."

"Dr. James is en route," Lori said, her arm covering her nose and mouth. "Crime scene techs just rolled up."

With the handkerchief pressed to her nose, Jess walked closer to the body lying in the middle of the kitchen on the classic black and white checked linoleum floor. Edna's head had been bashed. Considering the advanced state of decomposition, Jess could only assume that she'd been murdered the same day she'd made the call to her friend. Chances were she'd been forced to make the call and then bludgeoned to death.

"If Bruhn's keycard and ID are here, we haven't found them," Harper said, confirming Jess's conclusions as to why the lady was dead.

"At least now we know how Spears managed to smuggle Nina out of the clinic." Jess walked to the back door and opened it to let some air in.

"Looks nothing like North's MO," Lori noted. "Her mouth isn't sutured and there aren't any visible signs of strangulation." She shrugged. "Unlike the Dority murder, he had all the time in the world to follow his usual pattern."

"Nothing like Spears's work either," Jess noted. "Since North didn't send a selfie with this victim to his sister, I'm betting this isn't his kill."

"So we have at least one more active follower out there," Hayes suggested.

"Looks that way, Lieutenant," Jess agreed. "For that matter, North may have had assistance with all the bodies we've been finding the past few days."

She surveyed the kitchen. Nothing looked disturbed. It was the same throughout the small home. Everything appeared to be in perfect order, except for the lady of the house. "Let's have one last walk through to see if there's a message from Spears we missed somewhere."

That was the thing about Nina's disappearance. Why hadn't Spears sent Jess a message or made a move? What was he waiting for? Nina had been missing for six days. Spears obviously had a plan that involved her.

Maybe Nina was his escape plan.

If that was the case, then she was still alive.

The only question was for how long.

5:50 P.M.

On the way home Jess reminded herself that on some level she had known all along that Nina was with Spears, and still she wished the news had been different. There was no consolation in discovering that her deduction had been correct. In fact, it made her sick to her stomach to think of how Nina might be suffering with no understanding of what was happening to her.

"Chet mentioned that Mr. Burnett's going home tomorrow," Lori said.

Jess pushed aside the troubling thoughts and managed a weary smile. "He is. He's recovered amazingly well."

"And Chad is doing great," Lori went on, sounding almost too chipper. "He'll be back to work before we know it. Any word yet on how soon Chief Burnett will be reinstated?"

"Chad is recovering very nicely." Jess was so pleased about his progress. "I'm not sure a date has been set for Dan's reinstatement. There's still the Allen case to deal with, you know."

"You think Spears or one of his followers killed Captain Allen?"

"I don't know. I'm leaning more toward Lopez." Leonardo Lopez, one of the most powerful drug lords on the west coast and whose children had wreaked havoc in Birmingham, had sent word to Jess that her trouble in the BPD had been taken care of. "Spears loves watching me squirm. Why help me out by getting rid of Allen?"

"Good point," Lori noted.

The silence that lingered for the next several miles had Jess wishing Lori would just say whatever was on her mind. She had a feeling all the questions were about avoiding a discussion of the proposition to bait Spears. Lori hadn't said a word on the subject since they left the house on Argyle Drive this time yesterday. Maybe she had decided Jess's plan for trapping Spears was not such a smart move. Maybe Spears wasn't the only one whose desperation was showing.

Jess had to admit the idea was pretty reckless.

As Lori turned onto Conroy Road, she finally spoke again. "In case you haven't noticed, Clint seems to be trying a little harder to get along the last couple of days."

Jess had noticed. "I'm glad to hear it." After all the friction between Hayes and the rest of the team she was beginning to think bringing him on board had been a mistake. With any luck he'd learned his lesson.

Right then and there Jess decided she had made a mistake putting the burden on Lori that her bait-and-trap plan involved. It wasn't fair to their friendship or to their working relationship. Jess wouldn't bring it up again. She would find another way.

Whatever else was wrong in the world, relief washed over Jess as they pulled into the driveway at her place and Dan's rented BMW was already there. Every minute they were apart she worried that Spears would make good on his threats about Dan. Her BPD surveillance detail parked behind the BMW.

Jess reached for the door handle. "Goodnight, Lori, I'll—"

"I thought about what you said," Lori offered before Jess could finish.

"And?" A mixture of hope and dread welled inside Jess.

"You're right. If we don't do something soon, Spears may disappear. We can't let that happen."

"You're sure about this?" Jess needed her to be sure. She was asking a hell of a lot.

Lori nodded. "We'll figure out a plan tomorrow."

"Tomorrow." Jess got out of the car without saying more. Her pulse was racing, but they both needed to think about the next step before taking it.

"Night," Lori called after her.

Jess waved and headed for the stairs at the far end of the garage that led up to her apartment. She slowed. Odd that the garage's overhead door was open. Her landlord never left it open unless he was working on a project.

"Jess!"

Startled, her hand instinctively dove into her bag. George Louis emerged from the shadows of the garage, careful to stay near the wide-open doorway. Bear squirmed in his arms. Jess relaxed a little even if her heart was still thumping. "Is everything all right, George?" She rubbed the puppy's back. "What's Bear doing out here with you?"

George looked toward her apartment before meeting her gaze. "I'm not sure." He backed deeper into the garage and motioned for Jess to join him. The puppy struggled to break free of his hold.

Her instincts going on alert, she kept her hand in her bag, her fingers wrapped around the butt of her Glock as she stepped into the garage. "Is something wrong?"

"When he—Dan—came home," George whispered, "he sent the officer who'd followed him away."

An uneasy feeling curled in Jess's belly. "That was fifteen, twenty minutes ago?" Dan had called her when he arrived home. He had known she was right behind him. Usually his detail was dismissed once they were both home, though it wasn't unusual for Dan to dismiss his a little early.

George nodded. "Yes, about fifteen minutes ago."

Working hard not to show her impatience, she prompted, "Did you see or hear something that concerned you after the BPD cruiser left?"

He nodded again. "A woman came."

Tension fired through Jess. "How did she get here?" There was no extra car in the drive or on the street.

George shrugged. "She walked, I guess."

Jess withdrew her Glock. George's eyes rounded. "Describe this woman to me."

"Well, I don't know…"

Worry gnawing at her, Jess rummaged for her cell phone next. "What was she wearing? What color was her hair? Was she tall or short?" *Dammit!* Icy fingers of fear tightened around her throat. Why couldn't she find her damned phone? *There.* She grabbed it and fixed her attention back on her landlord.

George blinked a couple of times and appeared to gather his thoughts. Jess wanted to shake the information out of him.

"She was taller than you. Brown hair. Thin. She wore a yellow dress or gown, she looked disheveled." He rubbed his free hand over his face and adjusted his glasses. Bear tried to wiggle loose. "And she wasn't wearing any shoes."

Oh hell. Jess hit Lori's number. "Okay, George, I need you to take the puppy in your house and stay there until I tell you it's safe to come out again."

"But…but…"

"Go, George." Lori's voice echoed from the cell. "Lori, I need backup. *Now.* And an ambulance. I believe Nina Baron is in my apartment." Jess ended the call. George still stood there, staring at her. "George, please, go inside."

She started out of the garage.

"Oh my," George groaned, causing Jess to turn back. "She…she was carrying something. It might have been a gun."

Jess glared at him. "What?"

"I…I didn't put it together until you…" He gestured to the weapon Jess held.

"Go inside," she ordered.

Jess left her bag on the ground and moved around the corner of the garage. She flattened against the building, put her finger against her lips, and then motioned to the two officers in the cruiser to join her.

When the officers had hustled over to her, she didn't waste any time. "There may be an armed female inside with Chief Burnett." Both officers visibly tensed. "I can't confirm, but I believe it may be Nina Baron. I've called for backup. Officer Wade, I want you to stay here and wait for their arrival." Wade nodded and took a position at the corner of the garage.

Jess turned to the other young man who reminded her of Cook. God, had she ever been that young? "Officer Brashier, you come with me."

"Yes, ma'am."

When they reached the stairs, Jess whispered, "I'm going first. There's a motion sensor six steps up. It's impossible to bypass it so we need to cross it at the same time so whoever is in there thinks it's just me. Stay behind me and stay down," Jess ordered.

The young man shook his head. "No way, ma'am. I go first."

Jess appreciated his chivalry, but there was no time. "If Nina Baron is inside, she's a paranoid schizophrenic who's been off her medications and she may be armed. We have to approach with extreme caution. Since she and I have met, she needs to see my face, not yours. Under no circumstances are you to do anything to harm her, do you understand me?"

"Yes, ma'am."

Jess shook her head. "Wait. This won't work. There's a monitor, Brashier, if she sees you, I can't predict what she'll do."

"No problem. You go up the stairs. Take your time. I'll go up the back of the stairs."

Jess frowned, and then she realized what he meant. He would climb up the support structure that held up the stairs. Why the hell didn't she think of that?

"Just don't break your neck," she warned, "I've spent too much time in hospitals lately."

He nodded and hurried to get into position.

Jess took a breath and walked to the stairs as she always did. She sent Lori a text and then entered her number once more. Jess put the phone on speaker so Lori could hear and tucked it into her bra. She hated skirts and jackets without pockets. Why in the world she ever bought this one she would never know.

She took her time climbing the steps. Her mind conjured up all sorts of horrific images of what she might find inside. Forcing them away, she focused on how she might approach Nina. Would Nina recognize her from the Labor Day barbecue at her parents' home?

As Jess reached the landing, Officer Brashier came up and over the banister just behind the glider George had given her. Brashier flattened against the wall next to the hinge side of the door. Jess reached for the knob, but the cocky young cop was too quick, he threw himself in front of her and had the door open in a heartbeat.

As her eyes took in the scene beyond the cop's shoulder, Jess's breath left her in a rush. Dan was on his knees, his head down. Nina stood over him, the barrel of the weapon in her hand mere inches from his head.

"Drop the weapon," Officer Brashier ordered. His weapon leveled on Nina.

"Don't shoot," Dan shouted, his voice hollow with something like defeat. "Whatever you do," he pleaded, "don't shoot her. Go back outside. Please, Jess, both of you, go back outside."

"Stand down, Brashier," Jess ordered, her heart threatening to burst from her chest. When this was over, she was going to remind him how the chain of command worked. "Wait outside."

He looked at her, his eyes as wide as George's had been. Just her luck to get a rookie who wanted to be a hero and who was also scared to death. He lowered his weapon, his hands shaking.

"Outside," she snapped.

Jess turned her attention to the woman who hadn't spoken. Nina hadn't moved. She stood statue still, staring down at Dan or at the weapon she held clasped in both hands.

With a steadying breath, Jess dared to move a step in their direction. "Nina, do you remember me?"

"No!" Nina shouted without looking at Jess. "Leave us alone!"

"It's okay, Nina," Jess assured her. "I'll stay right here."

"Dan?" Nina uttered an anguished sound. "I have to…do this. I have to…"

"You don't have to, Nina," Dan said gently, keeping his head down. "Whatever is wrong, we can fix it."

Nina glanced at Jess. "Who are you? No one else can be here!"

"I'm Jess, Nina. Remember, I saw you at your family's barbecue a few weeks ago. You looked so pretty."

"Make him leave. Make him leave now!" Nina glanced toward the cop standing on the landing behind Jess.

"Whatever you want, Nina." Jess kept her attention steady on the other woman and her grasp tight on her weapon, but she didn't take aim. The last thing she wanted was to make her feel threatened. "Officer Brashier, I'd like you to leave now. Close the door behind you, please."

"Chief Harris, I—"

"Do it!"

"Yes, ma'am." Brashier took his time, but he did as Jess ordered.

"Is that better, Nina?"

She looked at Jess then. "Are you Jess?"

Jess smiled, her lips trembling in spite of her best efforts. "That's right. It's nice to see you again."

Nina blinked, clearly disoriented. She turned her attention back to Dan. "Shut up! I don't want to hear them anymore."

"Jess," Dan pleaded, casting her a look that begged for her to understand, "go, please. Nina and I will work this out."

"Can't do that," Jess said softly. She wished her palms would stop sweating.

Nina shook her head. "Why are you doing this, Dan? Why do you want to hurt my family?"

"I would never hurt your family, Nina. Please put the gun down. You know me. I would never hurt you or your family."

It took all the strength Jess could rally to ignore Dan and to stay focused on Nina.

"I have to do this," Nina cried. "I have to." She shook her head again as if to clear it. "He said to wait for Jess. Are you Jess?" She glanced at Jess. Her arms trembled a little from holding the weapon so tight.

Fear pumped a little faster inside Jess. "Yes, I'm Jess. Dan is your friend, Nina. You don't want to hurt him."

"No! He left me when I needed him most. I have to do this and Jess has to watch. That's what I have to do. Yes." She nodded as if agreeing with a voice only she could hear. "Dan will hurt my family." Her whole body trembled this time. "Yes, I have to stop him."

"Nina," Dan said gently as he dared to turn his face up to hers, "please listen to me. I would never hurt you or your family. The man who told you this is a liar. Look at me, Nina. Please, just look at me. You know me."

"Keep your head down!" Nina's whole body seemed to shake now. "I can't look at you!"

Jess's stomach clenched as she considered her limited options. There was no stopping this tragedy from playing out. One by one she shut down her emotions and narrowed her senses to the moment— to Nina.

"He said Dan would hurt my family." Nina tilted her head as if listening. "Yes. I understand. Yes. He said I have to do it. I have to wait for Jess. Jess has to see." She glanced at Jess. "Are you Jess?"

Dan reached for Nina.

Jess flinched.

"Don't touch me!" Nina shoved the gun in his face and waved it awkwardly. "Don't touch me!" She shook her head. "I can't! I can't!" She went completely still, her finger curling on the trigger. "Please stop. I don't want to…no…please…"

"Nina." Jess stepped forward, drawing her attention.

"Don't come any closer!" She tilted her head again. "Yes. Yes. I know what to do."

"Nina," Jess repeated, louder this time. "I can get Sylvia on the phone right now and prove to you that your family is safe."

Nina's lips trembled. "Where's Dan?" Her face twisted with pain. "He said Dan would've come back to me if not for you. Now he's going to hurt my family."

"He's using you to hurt Dan, Nina. Please put the gun down."

Nina froze. "Dan?"

"I'm here, Nina." Dan lifted his face to hers once more. "Please put the gun down."

"I can't. I can't do it. I can't." Nina abruptly shifted her weapon toward Jess and backed away from Dan. "This is *your* fault."

Jess was aware of Dan's voice as he pleaded for Nina to look at him. *This was his fault, he urged. Don't hurt Jess.* Tightening her grip on her Glock, Jess took aim. "Put your weapon down, Nina," she heard herself say in a voice so detached she hardly recognized it as her own.

Nina steadied her aim and in that instant Jess understood how this was supposed to go down.

Dan hurled his body at Nina.

Jess dove for the floor as the distinct click, click, click echoed in the room.

The door burst open and her team rushed in.

"You okay, Chief?" Lori demanded as she reached for Jess.

Her head was spinning, but otherwise Jess felt reasonably sure she was fine. "I think so." Lori helped her to her feet. She would be sore in the morning from taking that dive.

Across the room, Dan held Nina in his arms as she sobbed. "It's over now. Everything will be okay," he promised. He made soft soothing noises to comfort her, but his eyes and the worry there was on

Jess. She tried to reassure him with a smile but her lips did little more than tremble.

Her hand shaking, Jess stared at her Glock. The urge to vomit hit like a kick to her stomach. She took a deep breath and steadied herself. "Detective Wells, call Dr. Baron. Let her know Nina is here."

As Lori made the call, Harper and Hayes secured the scene.

Jess struggled to regain her composure as Harper picked up the weapon Nina had dropped. "You sure you're okay, Chief?" He surveyed Jess.

At this point, she realized there was no simple answer to that question. "I'm getting there."

Harper checked the chamber and then the clip. "Damn."

Jess met his surprised gaze. "What's wrong, Sergeant?"

"It's not even loaded."

You won't know who or what to trust, not even yourself.

Spears's words echoed in Jess's head. He'd set this up, counting on what any good cop would do. "He wanted me to kill her."

How would Dan have ever looked at her again if she had killed Nina? Jess's heart slammed hard into her sternum. Or if she had allowed Nina to shoot her, risking the life of the child she carried.

As if he'd sensed that she needed him, Dan ushered Nina down on the sofa and covered her with his jacket, then he came to Jess and pulled her into his arms. "We're okay, baby. We're all okay."

Jess closed her eyes and leaned into his chest. He was right. They were okay.

For now.

CHAPTER TWENTY-ONE

UAB HOSPITAL, BIRMINGHAM, 7:00 P.M.

Jess waited outside the room where Nina and her family, including Dan, were gathered. They'd wanted her to join them, but it felt wrong. Nina didn't need the added confusion and uncertainty Jess's presence might trigger.

Other than the bruises on her wrists and ankles where she had been restrained, Nina was unharmed…physically. It would take time to determine the damage to her fragile psyche.

He said Dan would've come back to me if not for you.

Closing her eyes, Jess pressed her forehead against the cool wall. She fought hard to keep the tears back. It was ridiculous to react this way. Nina had only been repeating what Spears had recited to her, no doubt over and over until she could no longer decipher the difference between the truth and his ugly words. She'd lost all touch with reality. The voices in her head had driven her. Even then she had fought valiantly. Jess had seen firsthand her struggle. Nina hadn't wanted to hurt anyone.

"You okay?" Lori placed her hand on Jess's shoulder.

Jess took a deep breath and nodded. She'd lost count of the number of times she'd been asked that question. "I am. Yes." Incredibly, she kept the tears at bay.

"You saved her life. Spears was counting on your cop instincts making you pull that trigger. He underestimated you."

Jess finally allowed her gaze to meet Lori's. The words she'd held inside for the past hour and a half spilled out of her. "Nina pulled the trigger of her weapon. *Three times.* I risked the life of my child because I couldn't shoot her before she attempted to fire at me." She could only imagine how Dan would feel when he had time to consider how she had reacted.

"Even if the weapon had discharged, Chief Burnett—"

Jess held up a hand to stop her friend. "I know. There was a strong probability she wouldn't have hit me anyway." Jess fought for a decent breath. "But I took the chance. I keep telling myself I did it because I understood in that final moment what Spears wanted me to do. He wanted me to kill her and I couldn't do it."

Lori hugged her. "You did the right thing."

"Oh my God. I got here as fast as I could."

Jess and Lori pulled apart at the sound of Gina Coleman's voice.

She hugged Jess. "Nina's really okay?"

Difficult as it was, Jess summoned a smile. "Physically she's fine. We don't know about the mental abuse. Spears did a serious number on her. She was off her meds for almost a week." Jess couldn't talk about the details just now—not and hold herself together.

Gina pressed her hand to her chest. "Thank God. This has been a nightmare for Nina and the Baron family."

"I should check in with Sergeant Harper," Lori offered. "I'll be just down the hall."

Jess nodded. She could not wait to get out of here. She hated the way hospitals smelled. She hugged her arms around her middle.

"You sure you're all right, Jess?" Gina rubbed Jess's arm. "You're white as a sheet. Can I get you something?"

Jess shook her head. "I'm fine, really."

What a lie. She was so very far from fine. No point pretending anymore.

The door opened and Dan stepped into the corridor. Like Jess, he looked as if he'd stumbled from a war zone.

"Gina." He flashed that smile of his that never failed to make Jess's knees weak. "You should go in. I'm sure Sylvia will be glad you're here."

Gina hugged him. "You need to take Jess home. She looks ready to collapse."

Dan pulled Jess against him. "That's exactly what I'm going to do." He smiled down at her. "I told Sylvia you'd catch up with her tomorrow."

Jess nodded. She didn't trust herself to speak.

When Gina had slipped into Nina's room, Dan turned a worried face to Jess. "We're going home and talking about what happened."

Jess pulled free of his hold. "Sure."

She called a goodbye to Lori as she headed for the elevator. Dan did the same. Jess couldn't look at him as they left the hospital. She didn't want to see the contempt that would eventually fill those blue eyes.

She hadn't protected their child.

9911 CONROY ROAD. 8:30 P.M.

As soon as Dan had the door open, Bear burst out of the apartment. He was so happy to see them. His excitement almost made Jess smile.

"I'll take him for a walk." She needed some air.

Dan tossed his jacket aside. "I'll come, too."

"No, you…you can set the table." They'd picked up Chinese take-out on the way home. Jess should be starving, but all she felt was sick to her stomach.

Dan reached for the leash. "I don't think so."

Jess took the leash from him. "There are two officers right outside and I'm only walking around in the yard."

He made a face. "Take your Glock."

Jess dug it from her bag, the puppy trying to help. "Got it." She tucked it in her waistband and smoothed her jacket over it.

"You might need this." He thrust a doggie bag at her.

"Thanks."

"Jess."

She'd almost made it out the door. She didn't look back. "Yeah?"

"You did the right thing. You trusted your instincts and Nina's alive because you did."

"Thanks."

Tears blurred her vision. She fought to hold onto the leash as she moved down the stairs. When he'd had time to think, Dan wouldn't see it that way. He would be angry and rightly so.

"Where're we headed, Chief?" an officer called to her.

She waved him off, couldn't talk to anyone right now.

Dusk had chased the sun away. Jess was glad. Maybe George wouldn't spot her out here and come to chat. Her chest felt so tight it was almost impossible to get air into her lungs. Her stomach was churning.

She was a mess.

The sound of gravel crunching had her turning to see who had pulled into the driveway. Buddy Corlew. By the time he'd climbed out of the black Charger the two officers were already approaching him.

God, would her life ever be normal again?

Jess almost laughed. Had it ever been normal? She had no idea who her father really was—good guy or a cold-blooded killer? Did he and her mother die in an accident or were they murdered? She'd spent her entire adult life studying and chasing evil. How the hell could she expect normal?

Buddy swaggered over. "Hey, kid. Why aren't you answering your phone?"

"It's inside." Probably still on vibrate. Bear tried his best to get away from Jess and greet Buddy.

Buddy scrubbed the fur behind his ears. "How did this happen?" He jerked his head toward the dog.

Jess shrugged. "He just showed up and decided to adopt us." She searched Buddy's face. "What's up?" If Buddy had carved time out of his night to drop by something was definitely up.

"I had a visitor today."

Jess held tighter to the leash as Bear tugged against it. "And?"

"John Kurtze. He claimed to be the personal assistant to retired FBI Director Drummond. You know anything about him?"

"He retired before my time. He had a reputation for being a hard ass. Started several ground-breaking programs." She shook her head. "I've never met him."

"Evidently, he knows you and he knew your father. His assistant warned me to stay out of it. He said you'd have your answers in time."

Jess wasn't sure whether to be relieved or not. "I'll ask Gant about him." The whole situation was strange. Could her father have been an agent with the Bureau? Or was he one of the killers they failed to catch?

"I heard about Nina Baron. You and Dan okay?"

That was it. She couldn't hold back anymore. All the emotions she'd put on hold burst forth. "No. I am not okay and I doubt Dan is either." She took a breath. "I'm pregnant, Buddy, and I need this Spears business to end. I need it to end soon."

"You're having a baby?" Buddy stared at her as if she'd just told him she was not only pregnant but that he was the father.

"Are you deaf?" she groused. "Yes, I'm having a baby."

Buddy grabbed her by the shoulders and pulled her against his broad chest. "Congratulations, kid. I better be invited to the wedding."

"Of course you'll be invited. I'm just a little overwhelmed right now."

"I know." He patted her back. "This bullshit needs to end. You deserve some damned peace."

She didn't mean to cry. Dammit. The tears wouldn't be kept at bay any longer. "I want that son of a bitch. I want to put a bullet between his eyes." She drew back and scrubbed at her cheeks with her free hand. "Tomorrow, you and I are going to make a plan to get him. Do you hear me, Buddy Corlew? We're going to trap Eric Spears with what we both know he wants."

"Jess," Buddy argued, "you're not thinking straight."

"Yes, I am."

Bear suddenly jerked loose and lunged away. "Bear!" Jess started after him.

"Hold on. I'll get him." Buddy took off after the puppy.

Jess wiped her face and shoved her hair back. She had to calm down. Being this upset wasn't good for the baby. She trailed after Buddy. The puppy was digging furiously at the flowerbed beneath George's kitchen window.

She couldn't wait to have her own yard. Having a pet changed everything. She could only imagine how much things would change when the baby came.

Buddy pulled the dog back and smoothed the dirt and mulch he'd disturbed. "Bad dog," he scolded.

"I'm sorry I fell apart on you." Jess felt like a pathetic child. She was stronger than this. *This* was exactly what Spears wanted.

"Come on." Buddy held the leash in one hand and put his free arm around her shoulders. "You just need a good night's sleep. I'll walk you to your door."

"You're a good friend, Buddy. I meant what I said. We will talk tomorrow."

Dan was at the bottom of the stairs when they reached the garage. "How's it going, Corlew?"

"It's going." He passed the leash over to Dan. "Congratulations. Jess just told me you two are getting married and having a kid, too."

Dan extended his free hand. "Thanks."

The two shook hands. Jess could only stare. Wow. Maybe there was hope that these two could be friends after all.

"Well, I've got a hot date waiting for me." Buddy gave Jess a wink. "Talk to you tomorrow, kid."

When he'd driven away, she and Dan climbed the stairs in silence.

Maybe she should go ahead and bring it up to get it over with. Why try to pretend it hadn't happened. Inside, Dan locked the door and set the alarm. She looked away from the place where he'd knelt on the floor while Nina held a gun to his head…just like ten years ago. How had Spears known? Had he read her medical file?

"We should eat before it gets cold." Dan removed the leash from Bear's collar.

Jess shrugged. "I'm not really hungry."

Dan walked toward her and those damned tears brimmed in her eyes again. He took her face in his hands. "Talk to me."

"I…" Her lips trembled and she had to take a moment. "I didn't protect the baby. If Nina's weapon had been loaded—"

Dan smiled down at her, his eyes suspiciously bright. "You're beating yourself up for no reason. You did the right thing. We both did."

"What if—?"

He touched his finger to her lips. "What if didn't happen and we don't need to think about that—*ever*."

"She blames me for what happened between the two of you." Her legs had started to tremble. She wasn't so sure she could trust herself to stay standing right now.

"Jess, that was Spears talking. Nina would never have said any of those things. She was an accomplished attorney with her own practice, but she wouldn't stay on her meds. Our marriage ended because it needed to end, not because of you or even me. We may never fully understand exactly what went wrong, but the family hopes the hospital in New York will be able to help her."

Jess bit her lips together and fought unsuccessfully to hold back the next onslaught of tears. "I guess you're right. It was just difficult to hear those things."

"Some of what she said was true," Dan confessed, his voice low and filled with hurt.

Jess searched his eyes. "What do you mean?"

"Jess, I've spent my whole life in love with you. It was never going to work with anyone else because you are the love of my life and, until the day I die, I will love you with all that I am. I couldn't love anyone else the way they deserved to be loved."

Jess reached up and caressed his strong jaw. Her lips trembled into a smile. "I think we might have to reheat dinner…*later*."

He kissed her so tenderly her whole body wept with need. When her knees would have buckled, he swept her into his arms and carried her to the bed. He took her Glock and placed it on the nightstand, and then he started to undress her. She slipped the buttons of his shirt free and bared his chest to her desperate hands. The heat of his skin took her breath.

God how she loved this man.

He unzipped her skirt and let it fall to the floor. She shoved his shirt off his strong shoulders. While he unfastened her bra, she removed his belt. His trousers and boxers were next. He dragged her panties down her thighs and she stepped out of them.

They climbed into bed together. Across the room she was aware the puppy was into something—their dinner probably—but she couldn't have stopped touching and kissing Dan if her life had depended on it. The feel of his hands on her skin and his lips on hers was all she needed. He kissed his way down her body, hesitating on her belly to pay special attention there. With his hands and mouth he loved every part of her, bringing her to the very edge of her sanity.

It wasn't until he was deep inside her that she felt whole again. The voices and images of the day slipped away and there was only the two of them.

She held on as long as she could. To let go would allow reality to creep back in and reality was too terrible…

Spears was still out there.

CHAPTER TWENTY-TWO

"I can't believe the Court changed the date of the custody hearing without telling anyone," Jess huffed as she hurried up the steps.

"Clerical error," Lori said, keeping time with Jess.

"I'm glad Lil had the foresight to call and confirm the time." Jess certainly hadn't thought to verify the date and time of Maddie's hearing. The adoption would take time, but today was about custody until then. It was a formality really, but it had to be done.

Lori opened the door for Jess. "You have been a little busy."

Jess couldn't argue with her friend's reasoning. With the hearing this morning there had been no time to discuss the plan to trap Spears. Jess was beginning to think fate was trying to tell her something about that idea.

"I'm glad you're feeling better today."

"Me, too," Jess admitted, the heels of her shoes tapping on the marble floor. She had to give Dan credit. He'd helped her work through it. Her body still tingled when she thought about last night. Making love with Dan had healed the wounds of the day. No one else had ever been able to soothe her that way.

"Looks like they've already started," Lori whispered as they approached the courtroom where the hearing was scheduled.

Dammit. How could she be late for Maddie's custody hearing? *Deep breath.* Jess reached for the door, opened it, and came face to face with her sister who was in tears.

"What happened?" Jess demanded. She looked from her sister to her brother-in-law.

"Maddie's ours," Blake announced with a broad smile.

Lily threw her arms around Jess and sobbed like a child.

"For heaven's sake, Lil," Jess fussed, battling her own tears. "I'm not supposed to cry today."

Blake ushered them into the corridor and toward the doors Jess and Lori had only just entered. "We can pick her up at five this evening."

"We're having a dinner in her honor this Saturday," Lil said, wiping her eyes. "You and Dan have to come."

"Well, of course," Jess fretted. "I'll drop by and see her tonight, too. If that's all right." If her sister had special plans for the three of them Jess certainly understood.

"You know Maddie will want to see you. Bring Dan, too."

"It's a date," Jess promised. She chose not to remind her sister that if there was a murder or another move by Spears she might not be able to come by either night. Why ruin this special moment with reality?

Lil gave Jess another hug. "We have to go. We're getting Maddie's room ready."

Jess smiled as she watched Lil and Blake rush away like newlyweds expecting their first child. This was a big leap for the empty nesters.

"We have a few minutes," Jess checked her cell, "let's drop by the hospital and visit Cook." She'd been too upset to see him last night. He was out of ICU now. In another week he'd be home.

Lori suddenly stepped in front of her. Jess bumped into her back.

"Hold on," Lori warned.

A long black limo had stopped on the street in front of the courthouse steps. Jess and Lori had stalled about midway down.

A rear door opened and a man emerged.

Gant.

"We need to talk, Jess."

Jess moved down the final few steps separating them. "What's this about?"

"Let's take a ride. I'll take you back to your office when we're done. Detective, you can wait for Chief Harris at her office."

"I'm sorry, sir, but I can't do that. Wherever Chief Harris goes, I go."

Jess bit her lips together to hold back a smile.

"Jess?" Gant looked to her as if he expected her to handle the situation.

"Detective Wells goes with me."

Gant moved to the front door. "Have it your way. Detective, you can ride in the front with the driver."

"Happy to, sir."

Lori climbed into the front seat.

Gant gestured for Jess to step into the passenger compartment. When she ducked her head inside she drew up short. Two distinguished looking gentlemen sat in the seat facing Jess. One looked to be in his mid-seventies while the other was ten or so years younger. Jess settled into the luxurious leather seat opposite her hosts. Gant scooted in next to her.

"I've been looking forward to meeting you, Jess," the older man stated as the car moved away from the curb. "Winston Drummond." He gave her a nod. "This is my assistant John Kurtze."

"Mr. Kurtze smiled. It's a pleasure to meet you, Jess. I've heard a great deal about you."

So this was the man who'd warned Buddy to keep his nose out of the past. "Thank you," Jess allowed before turning to Gant. What the hell did he have to do with this? "You want to let me in on the secret now?"

"Director Drummond generously offered to come here in person to answer some of the questions you have about your father."

A new kind of tension moved through Jess. "What do you know about this?" She'd known Ralph Gant for nearly twenty years. She had worked directly for him for more than half that time. They'd never once discussed her parents.

"Agent Gant knows only what I told him," Drummond interjected.

Jess turned her attention to the man whose painting hung in the hallowed halls of the FBI headquarters in Washington, D.C. Retired Bureau directors were forever referred to as director. "All right then, why don't you tell me about my father?"

"Back in the seventies and eighties we were still fighting the Cold War on an international front. Here at home we were learning just how good the Russians were at planting sleeper agents. We were fighting a war on Main Street that never made the news. It was our most classified operation."

Jess couldn't see what any of this had to do with what her father had gotten himself into with the Brownfields and she said as much.

"We were trying out a very rudimentary form of homeland security. It was, of course, significantly smaller and far less sophisticated. We turned everyday citizens into watchers. Your father was one of our watchers. We had no idea when we embedded him that he would uncover some of the most evil elements we would encounter in those early

229

days—none of which had anything to do with the Russians." He gave a small wry laugh. "I'm afraid our methods weren't as well-honed back then and we lost many recruits. The operation was eventually pronounced a failure and shut down. As much of an overall failure as it was, it wasn't all bad, Jess. We gained a deeper understanding of the criminal element thriving in our communities. Much of what we learned then helps us solve some of the worst crimes we face today."

"No one was ever supposed to know about people like my father," Jess surmised, emotions she couldn't begin to label expanding against her chest. "The families were just left in the dark." Her father had crossed that line by telling her mother anything at all, though Jess couldn't blame him. He'd been working blind. "Were these embedded agents properly trained?" She didn't care that skepticism weighted her tone.

"Training was minimal," Drummond confessed. "We had much to learn in those days."

"Where was backup when these people needed it?" She couldn't wait to hear the answer to that one. She crossed her ankles to prevent her foot from tapping. Dammit. Anger, hurt, injustice, and more of those feelings she couldn't readily identify twisted inside her.

Drummond held her gaze for a long moment. "There was never a plan for backup, Jess. These agents were on their own and that was understood from the beginning. Their job was simply to watch, but human nature got in the way and many became *involved* and ultimately paid a high price for that involvement."

White-hot fury rose inside Jess so swiftly she barely restrained it. "There must have been some required criteria to be a watcher. How was my father selected? Or did you just randomly select any father of small children to get himself killed?"

"Your father's work in sales kept him on the road," Drummond offered, choosing to ignore her remark. "No one was going to notice a change in his habits. He was reasonably well educated and had the right personality. It was all quite simplistic."

Jess fought for a deep breath. The sheer arrogance and indifference of the man was suffocating. The only way she would get the answers she needed was if she kept her cool. "How long was he a part of your program?"

"From the time you were about two years old."

"Until it killed him," Jess finished for him. Drummond clearly felt no remorse for what he had done. *Breathe.* "From the time my father became involved with the Brownfield family, he and my mother spent the rest of their lives looking over their shoulders. They died because of his involvement with that family. Wasn't it obvious he was in over his head?" Someone ordered her father to become more involved. Drummond had to know more than he was telling and she deserved answers. "Or was it just easier to ignore the situation? After all, Lee Harris was expendable. Who would ever know?"

"Jess," Gant cautioned.

"I'm afraid I have no other answers for you, Jess," Drummond announced with a patience that sounded more patronizing than tolerant. "What the watchers did went undocumented. There were no files. Whatever answers you've uncovered are likely more extensive than the few I have."

"So my parents lost their lives because your program was a failure," she threw back at him without any of the fake patience and kindness he used so patently. He was lying. He had to know more than he was sharing. The idea that he could look at her and lie so easily made her sick.

"You know how it works, Jess," Gant insisted. "The average citizen might not understand, but you do."

No. She didn't understand. "If you don't have any more of the answers I need, then we're done." She had no desire to sit here and listen to how proud she should be that her father had lost his life serving his country without the proper tools with which to do it and without any backup.

"I watched you and your sister, Jess," Drummond said. "When you chose a similar path as your father, I put in a good word for you. You did your father proud."

"Are you suggesting that you had some influence on my career with the Bureau?" Shock radiated through her. How dare he imply such a thing!

"After your father's brave sacrifice, I felt it was my duty to see that the right doors were opened for you—not that my influence was necessary. You managed quite well without any help from anyone."

Jess struggled to keep her outrage in check. "You're right, *sir*, I didn't need your help finding my place at the Bureau. But if you were so damned concerned, you might have thought about helping when my sister and I were being tossed from one foster home to the next. I'm confident my father wasn't expecting that to happen when he signed on for your program."

Drummond looked away. Apparently, he didn't have an answer for that one.

Jess turned to Gant. "When did you know about this?"

"I had no idea until this morning."

Enough. "Stop the car."

"Jess," Gant argued. "We can take you back to the courthouse."

"I said, stop the car!" She couldn't breathe.

Kurtze tapped on the privacy glass and motioned for the driver to pull over.

When the door opened, Jess realized there was one other thing the director needed to know. "You know, as a profiler I spent years studying evil and teaching others how to find it. Inevitably someone would ask what evil looked like. My answer was always the same. If they wanted to know what evil looked like they should look in the mirror." The fury she'd been restraining slashed through her. "Have you looked in the mirror lately, Director?"

Gant emerged and held the door for her. She stepped away from the limo and drew in a deep breath to clear her lungs of the deceit.

"I'm sorry you had to find out this way, Jess."

She turned to her old boss and shook her head. "I'm not. It just confirms the decision I made resigning from the Bureau. Goodbye, Gant."

Jess walked away from him, Lori at her side.

She was where she was supposed to be. The Bureau had taken all from her they were ever going to take.

"I know you'll tell me what happened back there eventually."

"I will."

"How are we going to proceed with our plan?"

Jess had a damned good idea. She surveyed the street. "We need a taxi to take us back to your car."

"Where're we headed?"

"The hospital. I want to talk to Rory Stinnett one last time before she's released. First though, we have to stop by the office. There's something I need."

UAB HOSPITAL. 10:50 A.M.

Rory Stinnett was not happy to see Jess. Her mother was even less happy.

"Mrs. Stinnett, your daughter is over the age of consent and this is police business. Why don't you go get a coffee and we'll be finished here by the time you're back."

"I'm calling our attorney," the mother threatened.

234

Jess kept a smile propped in place until the woman was out the door.

"I already told you everything I know," Stinnett insisted.

Lori took the manila folder she'd brought and went to the wall directly behind Jess. The wall Stinnett would have to stare at for the next few hours until she was released. Until Lori was finished Jess wanted the woman's attention on her. She handed Stinnett an eight by ten photo of Spears.

"Look very closely, Rory. Did you at any time while you were a hostage see this man?"

Stinnett held the photo by the very edges as if she feared touching any part of his face. She shook her head. "Nope. I never saw him."

Lori stepped to the side of the bed and gave Jess a nod.

Jess moved to the other side of the bed, giving Stinnett a clear view of the wall and the dozens of gruesome images posted there.

Stinnett gasped.

"All those women, including Presley Campbell, were victims of Eric Spears." Jess indicated the photo Stinnett held. "Each one was tortured relentlessly for days. Raped repeatedly and then murdered. This is the man you're protecting."

"I swear I can't remember," Stinnett cried. "I...I don't know!"

"As long as he's out there," Jess warned, "you will never be safe, Rory. No matter how you swear you didn't see him, he knows you saw him. He knows everything about you. That's how he chooses his victims. He knows where you live. Where you work. Who your friends are. He knows everything."

Stinnett burst into sobs.

Jess let it go there. She'd pushed her hard enough. "I'll just leave these with you so you can think about it for a while. Maybe you'll remember something."

Outrage pounding inside her, Jess left the room. The mother hurried back in to be with her daughter. The sound of her shouting followed them down the corridor.

"I think maybe momma might be upset with you."

"If we're lucky and her daughter talks, she'll thank me in the end." Jess stabbed the call button on the elevator. "Let's go see how many nurses have asked for Cook's number."

"Last count was five." Lori laughed. "The guy's going to get a big head."

Jess had a feeling all those cute nurses were wasting their time. Chad Cook was smitten with Dr. Sylvia Baron.

"I guess you're going to Roark's funeral?" Lori asked as they boarded the elevator.

"It's mandatory, but I'd go anyway. At some point in his career he was a good cop, before power or greed got the better of him."

"Guess so."

She and every other cop in the BPD owed Roark the respect due him for those years of dedicated service.

DEPRAVED

With Lily beaming, Maddie took Jess by the hand and led her to the stairs.

"Can Uncle Dan come see your room, too?" Jess asked the little girl.

Maddie looked over at Dan and then nodded.

Dan gave a nod to Blake and joined Jess and Maddie at the bottom of the stairs. "I would love to see your new room, Princess Maddie."

Maddie giggled and ran up the stairs.

Jess and her sister had taken a few minutes together while Blake and Dan helped Maddie make cookies—what a sweet mess that had been. Lily had been just as stunned to learn about their father's true occupation as Jess had been. Though many of the pieces were missing, the news provided some amount of closure. They'd shed a few tears and done a lot of hugging, but tonight was about Maddie.

Lily had taken the guestroom Jess had always used when she visited and turned it into a veritable wonderland. The walls were pink. Glossy white furniture and a bed with a frilly canopy filled the room. There were dolls, a dollhouse, and oodles of stuffed animals, along with a little table and tea set. It was incredible.

"This is the best room *ev'r!*" Maddie squealed as she jumped on the bed.

Jess sat down in one of the little chairs at the table. "I'd like some tea, please!"

Maddie bounced over and arranged the cups and saucers. She looked up at Dan. "You, too!"

Dan knelt next to the table. "Honey, I'm afraid I'm way too big for your chairs."

"You can be a giant!" Maddie's laughter tinkled around the room.

"Wait!" Jess stood. "I have to get my phone so I can take a picture."

"*Hur-ree* up!" Maddie ordered.

Jess paused at the door to look back. Maddie was serving tea to Dan. The way he smiled at the little girl made Jess melt a little inside. She couldn't wait to watch him play with their children.

All she had to do was protect him until this was over.

Tomorrow she and Lori would set a plan in motion.

CHAPTER
TWENTY-THREE

"Good morning, Tara."

The receptionist looked up and gasped. "Chief!"

Dan grinned. "How are you this morning?"

She smiled. "Much better now."

"Chief Black is expecting me."

"You know the way." She blinked rapidly to hold back tears.

Dan wanted to hug her. This had been Tara's first job out of college. She'd been so nervous on her first day. She and Dan had had a special bond since that same day had been his first as chief of police.

Dan's step felt lighter as he headed for his office. It wasn't official yet, but it would be soon. He had a tremendous amount to be grateful for this morning. His father was being released from the hospital today with an encouraging prognosis after having two additional stints put in place. His other wounds were healing nicely. Dan wanted his father around to play the role of grandfather. Nina was safe in another private facility until the transfer to New York. The family had decided to keep her close for a while given the trauma she'd just suffered.

Jess had saved Nina's life. He was certain Spears had intended for Nina to die and Jess to be the cause.

Dan checked his cell once more before stepping into the small waiting room outside his office. Corlew was supposed to have made contact with the cell number Spears used. Hopefully he'd heard something by now.

One way or the other, Dan intended to ensure Spears was taken care of permanently.

"Chief!" Sheila jumped up from her desk and came around to give him a hug. "I'm so glad you're here."

"It's good to be here."

"You go on in. Chief Black is waiting for you." Her eyes sparkled. "I believe he has some good news for you."

Dan gave her a smile and headed into his office. No matter how dire the situation had looked, he'd still considered this *his* office.

"Good morning, Dan." Harold stood at the head of the small conference table in the room. "Have a seat and we'll get started."

"Morning, Harold." Dan was struggling with the changes to his and Harold's relationship. He had known and trusted the man for many, many years.

This business had left a seriously bad taste in Dan's mouth. He was looking forward to putting it behind him.

When Dan had taken a seat, Harold settled into his. He clasped his hands atop a folder on the table. "I received an urgent call from the AG in Montgomery this morning."

"I'm assuming the call was related to Meredith." Meredith had left Birmingham a number of years ago to take a job at the state level on the governor's staff. Dan couldn't imagine a call from the AG's office having anything to do with him otherwise.

"It was indeed." Harold took a moment as if what he had to say was difficult for him. "Late yesterday afternoon the AG received a package Meredith Dority mailed, according to the postmark, the day before her murder."

Dan waited for the rest, his heart pounding. It hurt to think of Meredith being brutally murdered. To some degree Pratt was responsible for placing her in that position. Damn him and damn Eric Spears.

"Meredith had compiled a lengthy and well-documented history of Mayor Joseph Pratt's illegal activities. Everything from granting favors to friends to diversion of funds."

"Good God." Dan had known Pratt had skirted the edge in many ways. Hell, he'd kept Pratt out of trouble on more than one occasion, but he never suspected the trouble was illegal or ran this deep.

"Meredith acknowledged her part in covering up his activities, and she also completely exonerated you. She explained that Pratt had blackmailed her into making the allegations against you. Since Meredith helped support her mother, she feared losing her job so she went along at first. For whatever reasons she couldn't see it through. She'd planned to come forward the day she was murdered, but mailed the evidence to Montgomery just in case Pratt's influence in Birmingham might interfere with justice being served."

Dan shook his head. "This is unbelievable. I knew Pratt pushed the boundaries. Hell, we all knew that. I wouldn't have believed he'd go this far."

Harold pushed the folder across the table to Dan. "In light of this news and the fact that I just received a call from Lieutenant Colbert informing me that the IAB has cleared you of any misconduct, you are officially and immediately reinstated as chief of police." Harold stood and extended his hand. "Welcome back, Dan."

Dan rose and accepted his hand. "Thank you."

"I know these were trying times for us. I hope that we'll be able to get past any hard feelings."

"You did what you had to do, Harold." There was no need for him to bring up Roark or anything else. It was over now. IA would investigate Roark's activities, but the man was dead. Barring any accomplices, whatever other misconduct within the department he may have been involved in likely went to his grave with him.

"We both know Pratt will be stepping down."

"In my opinion," Dan wasn't going to pretend there was any love lost, "that's the best thing that could happen for Birmingham." The mayor would in all likelihood be prosecuted as well.

Harold nodded his agreement. "I've moved back to my office." Harold waved a hand to indicate the room. "It's all yours once more."

Dan put a hand on his arm, stopping him when he would have taken his leave. "I know things are tough at home, Harold. If there's anything I can do, please let me know."

Harold gave a nod and took his leave. Dan went to his window and gazed out at the city he loved.

It was good to be back.

"Chief."

Dan turned to find his secretary waiting at the door. "Yes, Sheila, come in."

"You have a visitor. Gina Coleman. She says it's urgent that she see you right away."

Worry furrowed Dan's brow. "Of course. Send her in."

Sheila disappeared and seconds later Gina strode through the door, not bothering to close it. Ever vigilant, Sheila pulled the door closed.

"Good morning, Chief of Police Burnett." Gina smiled as she paused in front of his desk.

"Good morning to you. What brings you here this morning?" He gestured to one of the wingbacks flanking his desk.

Gina chose a chair and got comfortable. "I'm here to discuss your future."

"Is that right?" Dan settled into his chair. It felt damned good to be back in this chair. "You're ready to get started on your feature story already?"

"Just a little preliminary research." She smiled. "I heard from one of my sources that Mayor Pratt is announcing his resignation today."

Dan laughed. He should have known Gina would have gotten wind of the news even before he did. "I have no comment, Ms. Coleman."

Gina grinned. "I'm not here about the story on Pratt, Dan."

"To see my smiling face then," Dan suggested with a grin.

"That's always a pleasure, but no. It's about your future, as I said."

"I can't wait to hear it then."

"Those in power in this city are preparing a proposition for you, Dan, and I'm here to make a deal for the exclusive."

He laughed. "I'm afraid you've lost me, Gina."

"You're going to be the next mayor of Birmingham, Dan, and I want that move to be the cherry on top of my exclusive on the making of the city's golden boy."

"Let's not get ahead of ourselves here." He was undeniably flattered, but that was a huge leap to make.

"My source is solid, Dan." Gina's expression dared him to doubt her.

"*If* that opportunity is presented to me, Jess and I will discuss it and go from there."

"Speaking of Jess," Gina went on in full journalist mode, "I'll want the wedding to be a part of my profile. I hear it's going to be in December at St. Paul's."

"You'll need to discuss including our wedding plans with Jess," he hedged.

Gina grinned. "Good thing Jess and I are friends." She stood. "I have work to do. Good day, Mr. Mayor."

Dan pushed to his feet. "I've only just been reinstated as chief of police."

Gina hesitated at the door. "The people of Birmingham love you, Dan. Mark my word, you will be our next mayor."

"You're assuming I would say yes."

"You'll say yes." She wiggled her fingers in a goodbye and walked away.

Dan turned back to his prized window. There was a lot of good he could do as mayor, but serving as chief of police was what he loved. More importantly, he and Jess were going to be newlyweds and parents. After all these years, this was finally their time. He wanted to enjoy that time. He wanted to be the hands-on father his had been. Jess had her doubts, but he knew she would be a wonderful mother.

The most important thing he had to do right now was to keep her safe—whatever it took. He withdrew his cell phone and checked his messages. Still nothing from Corlew.

Certainly before he could ponder his future career, he had to end Spears's reign of terror.

There was only one way to do that.

Find him and kill him.

CHAPTER TWENTY-FOUR

NOON

Jess, her bag weighing down her shoulder and her notes in a pile in her arms, rushed into the conference room. Thankfully, Dan had saved a couple of seats. She sat next to him and Lori scooted into the chair beside her. Gant stood at one end of the long conference table. He was already talking, but Jess had gotten here as fast as she could. She and her team had gone over Cook's apartment again. Then they'd walked through the reverend's house as well as the hotel room he'd used once more. The efforts had turned out to be a waste of time.

She and Lori hadn't managed to grab a moment alone to discuss their plan. Maybe when this conference was over there would be an opportunity.

"Glad you made it," Dan whispered with a teasing glint in his eyes.

"All I can say is this better be worth dropping everything and rushing over here," she whispered back.

Dan shrugged indicating he didn't know any more than she did.

As she organized her notes to give an update on where her team was on its part in the Spears's investigation, she couldn't help being disappointed that Rory Stinnett evidently hadn't been moved by Jess's dramatic plea for help. Giving her grace, the woman was traumatized. It might be months or years before she could talk about what she knew.

Gant was saying something about Spears. Jess stopped fiddling with her notes and listened up.

"Just an hour ago Rory Stinnett identified Eric Spears as the man who held and tortured her and the others at the Argyle Drive house. She also identified Quentin North as his accomplice."

Jess resisted the urge to smile. Evidently, she'd gotten through to the woman after all.

"Twenty minutes ago we issued a new BOLO for Spears and a gray Nissan Altima he commandeered."

"Spears stole a car? Why weren't we notified of this sooner?" Harold Black asked.

"Good question, Chief Black," Dan seconded. "If Spears is on the move, I should have been notified immediately. I have an obligation to my citizens to ensure they're protected. Leaving myself and the rest of this Task Force out of the loop is unacceptable, Gant."

Go, Dan! Jess wanted to hear the answer to this as well. More importantly, she wanted to get out of here. Spears was on the move. Time was running out for the move *she* wanted to make. She did not want him to disappear.

Gant braced his hands on the back of the chair in front of him. "We had to move quickly, Burnett. There was no time." When Dan would have lodged another argument, Gant went on, "Only moments ago, we received our first hit on the BOLO."

"Where?" Jess demanded pushing to her feet. "We should be there."

"I have a team en route to Finagin Airfield. A man matching Spears's description chartered a private plane."

"I need to be there," Jess argued. "We shouldn't be wasting time."

"I second that," Black stood. "We need boots on the ground."

Gant passed out an update containing the details of the stolen vehicle Spears was believed to be driving. Jess stared at his image. *You're not getting away, Spears.*

"We've grounded every private airfield in a hundred mile radius," Gant explained. "The airport, bus stations, and train station are on high alert. Spears is not leaving this city via public transportation."

Jess had worried he would disappear until things cooled off, only to reappear God only knew when and where. He'd done it before. Yet, until today, he'd seemed determined to finish this game, whatever the cost. He'd planned a big finale that included Jess. Except something had gone wrong.

"Amanda started a snowball effect."

When everyone in the room, including Gant, stopped talking and stared at her, she went on. "Amanda Brownfield gave us the information we needed to find him. Spears was so certain of her allegiance that he didn't see it coming. He wasn't prepared." Jess took a breath, the developing scenario gaining momentum, and pressed on. "Ego represents a large part of who Spears is, beyond being a sociopathic serial killer. He's brilliant and he's an extreme narcissist. The trouble is, he's also a perfectionist and obsessive. He rarely fails, but when he does it's unacceptable. His most recent attempts to accomplish certain goals have all failed, damaging his ability to focus and operate effectively. He has two choices before him now, lose or disappear."

Jess hesitated, the utter silence in the room compounding the burden of what she understood with complete certainty about Eric Spears. "Losing is unacceptable. If we don't find him before he gets out of this city, we'll never find him." Until he wants to be found, she kept to herself.

Everyone started talking at once.

Gant reached into his jacket pocket for his cell. Jess watched his face as he listened to the caller. "I'll be there in twenty minutes."

The room fell silent once more. Jess held her breath as she waited to hear the news.

"Spears abandoned the stolen car and took a hostage at the airfield when he learned the plane he'd rented wasn't going anywhere. According to witnesses on the scene, he left no more than fifteen minutes ago. Our people likely passed him en route. He's driving a FedEx van. The driver is with him."

"We need to lock down this city," Dan demanded. "I want him found."

Black nodded. "We'll make it happen."

The members of the Task Force hurried from the room, each BPD division chief already on his or her cell issuing orders.

Dan touched Jess's arm before she could get away. "I don't want you involved in this manhunt. If he believes we're closing in on him there's no way to know what he might do."

Jess counted to five before reminding Dan that she, like the other division chiefs, had a job to do.

"He's right, Jess." Gant joined their huddle. "You shouldn't be out there. He's made it clear for two months that he wants to end his game with you. Why risk giving him the opportunity?"

"I will not hide while everyone else in this department is out there risking their lives." She shouldered her bag and gathered her pile of notes. "If you'll excuse me, I have work to do."

"That's an order, Jess," Dan said before she got out the door.

She stared back at him, angry and frustrated and scared dammit. "Yes, sir."

"You are not to allow her out of your sight, Detective," Dan ordered Lori.

"Yes, sir."

When she and Lori were halfway to the stairwell, Lori asked, "So, what's the plan?"

Jess glanced over her shoulder. "We go back to the office and we do exactly what we were told."

"Okay."

When they reached the SPU office, Lieutenant Hayes and Sergeant Harper were walking the floor.

"We just heard they almost caught Spears at Finagin Airfield," Harper said. "What's going on?"

Jess dropped her load on her desk. "Sergeant, I'd like you and Lieutenant Hayes to report to Chief Black and help with the search for Spears. Detective Wells, contact one of the officers on duty at the hospital and let them know to be on high alert. I don't want that bastard getting anywhere near Cook. Make sure all the other details are on high alert." The women Spears had held hostage were all safely home now with their own surveillance details just as Lily, their Aunt Wanda, and Dan's parents were.

Harper looked from Jess to Lori and back. "What about the two of you?"

Jess knew what he was thinking. She and Lori were primary targets of Spears. Lori was the one who got away, so to speak, and Jess was his obsession. Who was going to watch after them?

"Sergeant, Detective Wells and I are perfectly capable of taking care of ourselves. I've been banned from the search and Detective Wells is my babysitter. Any more questions?"

Harper shook his head. "No, ma'am. We'll get going." He glanced at Lori one last time before leaving. "Be safe."

Lori nodded. "You, too."

Jess felt guilty that she hadn't urged Dan to be careful. What if something happened to him? She'd been too furious at him for giving that damned stand down order. He was a prime target, too!

"So." Lori turned to Jess. "What're we really doing?"

"We're going to offer Spears a way out?"

Lori walked closer to Jess's desk. "A way out of what?"

"Getting his head blown off by the first BPD cop who gets him in his sights."

"How do we do that?"

"Like this." Jess pulled out her cell phone and tapped the contact number Spears had used to taunt her in the past. She entered the message she wanted to relay then hit send before showing it to Lori.

Is this really the way you want it to end?

"He's probably taken yet another vehicle by now." Lori paced the floor. "He's too smart to stay in such a high profile vehicle. He'll look for something less conspicuous. If he disappears—"

Jess's cell chimed with an incoming text. She held Lori's gaze for a long moment before daring to check the screen.

Are you so sure this is the end, Jess?

Fear trickled inside her. "That's what I'm afraid of." She typed in a reply and hit send. *The game is over, Spears, unless you're willing to play on my terms.*

"That should prompt a reaction." Lori braced her hands on her hips and stared at Jess's phone in anticipation of a response.

The strained seconds ticked off and Jess could barely hold herself still. Maybe she was unraveling, too. Most would consider a move like this more than a little crazy.

We should talk, Jess.

"Holy shit," Lori murmured.

Name the time and place. Jess hit send, her hands shaking.

Three o'clock at the only place where you ever felt safe as a child.

"Do you know where he's talking about?"

Jess nodded. "The house in Irondale where Lil and I lived as kids before our parents died."

"Is there a chance in hell he'd really show up there?"

"There's only one way to find out."

TWENTIETH STREET SOUTH, IRONDALE, 2:55 P.M.

Lori parked her Mustang half a block down the street from the abandoned and dilapidated house where Jess had spent the first ten years of her life. She had pulled Harper and Hayes back to provide support here. As badly as she wanted to take Spears down, she wasn't a fool.

She stared at the only real home she'd known growing up. Everything after this had been misery.

"Do we wait out here or are we going in?" Lori looked from the quiet street to Jess.

Jess took a deep breath. She wished her heart would slow its pounding. "Everyone's ready?"

"Hayes is across the street with a sniper rifle," Lori confirmed. "Chet is ready to go in through the backdoor. Just waiting for your order."

"Then we're ready."

Lori clutched her arm. "You know that vest only allows so much protection. If he's in there or shows up…"

"I know."

"You shouldn't take the risk. Let me go. Think about the baby."

Jess smiled sadly. "I am thinking about the baby. If I don't end this, my baby will never be safe."

Lori nodded. "All right. Let's do this."

Once outside the car, Jess activated the links that allowed her to communicate with her team. Lori cast one last look at her.

It was now or never.

With each step she took Jess's pulse raced faster and faster. By the time she walked the short distance to the house she was sweating. Concentrating all her senses on every movement and every sound around her, she headed up the walk. Lori matched her stride. She climbed the few steps leading to the rickety porch. Childhood memories flitted through her mind. She and Lil chasing each other around the yard. Swinging as high as they could on that old swing set out back. Whispering to each other at night when the house was silent and all the tomorrows were full of promise.

Focus, Jess.

At the door she hesitated only for a second. "Going in," Jess murmured for the benefit of Hayes and Harper.

Weapon drawn, Jess pushed open the door.

Harper moved in from the back door.

"Kitchen is clear," echoed across the communication link.

Jess stalled in the living room.

"Living and dining rooms are clear," Lori said next.

Jess heard Harper call the all clear in the rest of the house, but she didn't move.

Spears wasn't here.

Was it possible he had been apprehended?

"You've got company." Hayes's voice resonated in the earpiece Jess wore.

Jess turned to the door. "Is it Spears?"

"Looks like a fed," Hayes said. "Female. She is armed and coming in."

The door burst open and Agent Vicki Hancock surveyed the room. "What the hell are you up to, Harris?"

"Following up on a lead," Jess said, annoyed at the idea that Gant or Dan or both had Hancock following her. "What're you doing here?"

"Following orders." Hancock holstered her weapon. "Gant instructed me to keep an eye on you."

"Has Spears been caught?" If not, Gant was misusing resources, in Jess's opinion.

"Nope. He killed the driver and abandoned the FedEx van. They lost him."

"Dammit." Where the hell was he? Unless someone spotted him or he stole another vehicle…he could get away.

"He's going to get away," Lori said, echoing Jess's thought, her voice uncharacteristically thin.

Before Jess could reassure Lori, her cell clanged that old-fashioned ringtone. She tugged it from her bag and checked the screen. George Louis. Why on earth would her landlord be calling?

Had Spears showed up at her apartment? It wouldn't be the first time a killer had showed up at her place.

"It's my landlord," she said in answer to the expectant gazes focused on her. "George? Is everything all right?" Jess held her breath. Part of her wanted so desperately to hear him say Eric Spears was having tea while he waited for her.

"I'm sorry to bother you," George said, "but I wasn't sure what to do. That terrible killer is all over the news and they were talking about you, too. I wasn't sure if I should bother you or not."

Jess reached for patience. "What's wrong, George?"

"A box was delivered to your door a while ago. I didn't think anything of it until I saw on the news where that awful Eric Spears had stolen a FedEx van."

Jess's heart banged against her sternum. "Did a FedEx van deliver the box?"

"Yes. Yes," George said. "It was one of those smaller vehicles like I saw on the news. Oh my, I don't know what to do."

"Is anyone there besides you, George?"

"No. No. I didn't see the driver and the van is gone. It was a while ago when it was here. I saw the box at your door and then the news and…"

"Don't go near the box, George. I'm on my way." Jess ended the call. "Sergeant," she said to Harper, "we need the bomb squad at my apartment as quickly as possible."

"Making the call now," Harper said.

Jess's phone vibrated. She jumped, almost dropped it, before glaring at it. What now? Her heart seemed to stop as she read a new message from Spears.

I'm cutting this game short. Perhaps we'll meet again one day. By the way, Dan sends his love. Too bad you couldn't be here, too.

Oh God. Fear coursed through Jess's body. "Dan is with him." She lifted her gaze to Lori's. "We need to find him."

Before it was too late.

CHAPTER TWENTY-FIVE

Dan parked at the curb in front of Gina's station. His surveillance detail eased into the spot directly behind his rental. He stopped at the driver's side door. "I'll only be a few minutes."

"We'll be waiting, Chief," the BPD officer driving assured him.

Dan headed for the station's main entrance. Gina had called and needed to see him immediately. She'd received a package with Helen Harris's music box inside as well as a note from Spears. Dan wanted to see it first, before he called Jess or Gant. If this was something else to hurt Jess, he wasn't sure he ever wanted her to see it. And if it was a trap he didn't want Jess anywhere near this station.

Eric Spears had hurt her enough.

"Dan!"

He stopped short of the entrance and scanned the small parking area to the right of the building. Gina waved to him from behind the wheel of one of the station's news vans. He changed course and hustled over to where she waited.

"What's going on?" She was the station's top reporter, maybe she had received a call since they spoke that couldn't wait.

"Jess called. She wants us to bring the music box to her."

"Jess? When did you speak to her? Where is she?" Had Jess told Gina about the music box? Possibly. They were friends. Right now Jess was supposed to be at the office, out of Spears's reach.

"She's at the apartment. We have to hurry, Dan. Hop in."

"Damn it." He didn't know why he'd expected Jess to listen. She had her way of doing things. He doubted that was ever going to change. Dan rounded the hood and climbed into the passenger seat. Gina hit the accelerator. The van rocketed out of the parking slot and away from the building.

"Did she say what she was doing at the apartment?" Dan clicked his seatbelt into place and checked the side mirror to see if his surveillance detail was following. The BPD cruiser remained parked behind his rental. He'd have to call and let them know where he was. He turned back to Gina. "Why is she at the apartment?"

Gina stared straight ahead as she merged into traffic. Her profile was rigid, her face pale.

"You need to tell me what's going on, Gina." If Jess was in trouble—

"Nice to see you again, Dan." Eric Spears leaned out of the shadows in the back of the van, his weapon settling against the back of Gina's head.

Gina gasped. "I'm so sorry, Dan." Tears slid down her face.

His hand went to the weapon at his waist.

"Now, now, Chief, let's play nice. I would hate to spew the lovely lady's brains all over the windshield."

Dan stilled. He didn't bother asking the bastard what he wanted. He knew the answer. Whatever he had planned he could forget about Dan cooperating. No way in hell.

"Let's take a little drive, shall we?"

Gina sobbed quietly, her hands clutching the steering wheel.

Dan thought of grabbing the wheel and crashing the van the way he had his SUV when Amanda Brownfield had tried to take him hostage, but Spears had his weapon jammed into Gina's skull. Dan couldn't risk her life. It was one thing to risk his own, but he wouldn't do that to her.

"This is between you and me, Spears. Let Gina go."

"I think not. Remove the weapon from your waist with your left hand and place it on the floor between the seats."

Dan reached for the weapon. Once he turned over his weapon—

"Think carefully, Dan. Ms. Coleman's life rests in your hands."

Dan lowered his weapon to the floor. Spears covered it with one leather-clad foot and dragged it away.

"You have my weapon. Let Gina go and let's finish this."

"What's the old saying?" Spears taunted.

He chuckled, the sound made Dan want to reach back and rip off his head.

"Ah, yes," Spears went on. "Be careful what you wish for, you might just get it. Your friend Mr. Corlew said you wanted a meeting. Welcome to the game, Dan."

Corlew had sent the message to Spears, but he'd never received a response.

Until now.

CHAPTER TWENTY-SIX

3:20 P.M.

"Any idea where we're headed?" Lori asked.

Jess and her team had loaded up in their respective vehicles and headed back toward Birmingham proper. She tried to think. Where would he take Dan? Worry and fear tightened her belly. They could be anywhere. "I should call Gant."

The clang of her cell startled her. She still had it clutched in her hand. *Buddy calling.* Jess forced a calm she didn't feel. "Hey." As hard as she tried to sound steady, the word shook. She cleared her throat. "What's up?"

"I'm not exactly sure, but I think Dan's in trouble."

More of that cold, stinging fear rushed through her veins. "I think he's with Spears." Jess bit down on her trembling lips. Jesus Christ she had to do something.

"That might explain what just happened," Buddy mused. "I followed him from BPD headquarters to the Channel Six Studios. He got into a news van with Gina Coleman. I'm tailing them now."

Relief so profound that Jess could hardly breathe flooded her. "You're following them?"

"Well, I was following you. That's what Danny boy ordered me to do, but that Agent Hancock got all up in my face and threatened to kick my ass and then sic Gant on me if I didn't back off. She said she was your shadow today. So I decided to follow Dan."

"Where are you?" Jess worked hard at keeping the tears from flowing and making her look like a fool.

"We just merged onto Tallapoosa Street from I-20."

"We're headed to Tallapoosa Street," she instructed Lori.

Lori passed the word to Harper and asked him to pass it along to Hancock who was bringing up the rear of this caravan.

"Stay on them, Buddy," Jess urged. Inside, she struggled with the next move. Did she risk Dan and Gina's safety by informing Gant of what they suspected was going down? "Did you get a visual on Spears?"

"Negative. Gina was already in the van when Dan got to the station. I can't say who's in there with them."

By the way, Dan sends his love.

Spears was with them. Jess didn't need a visual ID. "He's in there. About five minutes ago Spears sent me a text suggesting Dan was with him."

"This could get ugly fast, kid."

Buddy was right. "I'm putting you on speaker, Buddy." Jess tapped the screen. "Lori, call Gant and tell him...Spears has taken two hostages."

"We just took a right on East Lake Boulevard," Buddy spoke up. "Oh, hell. I know where this joker is going. He's headed to the East Side Heliport."

"Can he rent transport there?"

"East Side is a private heliport," Lori explained as she waited for her call to be answered. "He's either hired someone to get him out of here or he's planning to steal a helicopter."

"I'm backing way off," Buddy warned. "I don't want him to spot me."

Worry twisted inside Jess. "Don't lose them, Buddy."

Lori repeated the situation to Gant, the words tightening the vise of fear around Jess's chest.

Lori ended her call. "They're thirty minutes out."

Jess felt her hopes plummeting. Thirty minutes was a lifetime. "We're not waiting. Buddy, give me a rendezvous point."

"There's a gray building before you reach East Side Heliport. Meet me on the north end."

Jess ended the call. She sat very still, the life she and Dan had planned spinning past her eyes. Spears was beyond the point of no return.

He had nothing to lose.

Fifteen agonizing minutes later, Jess and her team, including Hancock, had reached Buddy's location and linked him into their communications.

Ever the prepared PI, Buddy had binoculars and all sorts of gear in a backpack.

"They entered the building two minutes ago," he said, bringing Jess up to speed. "Spears has a weapon. I didn't see anyone else. I think he's on his own."

"The heliport manager says there's no one on site today." Lori slid her phone into her back pocket. "He's en route with a key card for access."

"Heads up." Harper's voice came across the communications link Jess and her team were still using. "Another vehicle just arrived."

Harper had taken a position on the roof of the building where they waited. Hayes was inching his way toward the heliport headquarters.

Jess waited, blood roaring in her ears.

"One man," Harper said. "Caucasian. Blond hair. Thirty maybe. He's wearing a flight suit. I'm guessing he's the pilot Spears hired."

"Gant and the others are still ten minutes out," Hancock said. "We need to sit tight until backup arrives."

"That's a good idea, Agent Hancock," Jess said. "You sit tight. My team is going in."

"Gant's orders are to stay put until he gets here. You can't go in," Hancock argued. "It's too dangerous, Harris."

Jess looked her straight in the eye. "Watch me."

"Have it your way." Hancock shrugged. "I guess I'll just have to go with you."

It wasn't until they split up and started moving in that Jess realized she was still wearing her vest. Just as well, she decided. Saved her the time of dragging it on again.

"There's an entrance on the west end." Hayes voice sounded over the communications link.

"It'll be locked," Lori said. "The owner is five or so minutes away."

"Give me a minute to get there," Buddy said, his voice resonating across the link, "and I'll take care of that for you."

"Exigent circumstances," Hancock said when Jess glanced at her to see if she was going to challenge Buddy's offer.

Jess knew she liked this woman.

Hayes was waiting at the west entrance when Jess and the others arrived.

Buddy dragged the pack off his back and did a little scrounging around inside. He pulled out an electronic keycard decoder and tucked the card into the slot. Ten seconds later the lock disengaged.

If there was an alarm…Jess held her breath.

When the silence stretched on, they moved in.

The building was two stories. Harper, Buddy, and Hayes took the first floor.

Jess headed for the stairwell. Lori slipped ahead of her at the door and moved up the stairs first.

The stairs seemed to go on forever. By the time they reached the second floor, Jess's heart was pounding even harder. Lori cracked open the door and checked the corridor. Somewhere on this floor would be the access to the rooftop helipad.

The sound of raised voices echoed and then a scream rang out in the unbearable silence.

Gina.

Moving swiftly and quietly, Lori led the push toward the sound.

At the door marked roof access, Hancock took a look and then opened the door.

Gina lay on the floor at the bottom of the stairs. When she looked up, Jess pressed a finger to her lips. Gina had taken a hell of a tumble, but she was conscious and there was no blood. Thank God. Jess pointed to Lori and then to Gina.

Judging by the look Lori gave her she wasn't too pleased with the order to take care of Gina. There was no time to debate the decision.

Jess and Hancock moved up the stairs. At the door leading to the roof they paused to take stock of the situation.

"Chet and Hayes are on the way up." Lori's voice echoed in Jess's ear.

Jess eased the roof door open and had a look.

Spears had his weapon trained on Dan. Next to Dan, the pilot's hands were in the air. Jess imagined he'd wished a thousand times over that he hadn't taken this call. Jess held perfectly still. All three of the men were no more than ten yards away. If Spears glanced to his right he would spot Jess.

"I'll be sure to check on Jess and the baby," Spears was saying to Dan. "I'll drop by the lovely house you purchased and say hello." Spears shrugged. "I can be a very patient man. Perhaps I'll wait until the child is old enough to watch before killing Jess."

"You'd better shoot me now, you son of a bitch." Dan moved toward him.

Jess held her breath.

Spears took aim. "Good bye, Chief of Police Burnett."

"Drop your weapon, Spears," Jess shouted as she moved out the door and onto the roof. She quieted the emotions churning inside her and stopped, feet apart, weapon aimed at her target.

Spears smiled. "Oh, this is too perfect."

In the distance sirens wailed.

"Drop your weapon, Spears, or I will shoot," Jess repeated.

"You heard her, Spears." Hancock moved into position next to Jess. "Drop that weapon or you're a dead man."

Spears exhaled a dramatic sigh. "So here we are, Jess, at the end of our game." He didn't have to face her. His profile showed enough of his arrogant smile. "Any last words to say to the man you love?"

Jess stared down the sight of her Glock. She took a deep breath, released half of it. "Do you want pizza or Chinese for dinner?"

Before Spears could reply or make a move Jess pulled the trigger.

The bullet slammed into his brain just above his right ear and he dropped to the tarmac.

The blast from the discharge seemed to go on forever. After that the only sound was the wail of sirens growing closer and closer.

Dan was suddenly next to her, urging her to lower her weapon. Jess stared into his eyes and whatever strength had kept her steady vanished. She fell into Dan's arms and pressed her cheek to his chest. She needed to feel his heart beating.

The roof was suddenly crawling with cops, but all Jess could hear was Dan's voice whispering reassurances.

It was over.

Eric Spears was dead.

CHAPTER
TWENTY-SEVEN

"What do you suppose they're talking about out there?" Lil giggled and sipped her wine. "Maybe how lucky they are to have two beautiful, sexy ladies like us?"

Dan and Lil's husband, Blake, had taken the puppy out for a nice long walk and were now sitting on the landing having a beer. Maddie was sound asleep on the sofa. She looked like an angel.

Tonight had been about celebrating survival. Spears was dead. He would never haunt their lives again. There were no words to adequately articulate how relieved Jess felt. It had been a long day. There would be counseling sessions and an investigation of the shooting in her future, but Jess didn't care. It was over. Anyone who thought she might suffer any remorse or doubts about the decision to shoot Spears was wrong.

The package delivered to Jess's door had been their mother's music box. She couldn't understand why Spears would leave the package for her. Taking time to make the delivery with cops crawling all over the city looking for him didn't make sense.

Another mystery she might never be able to solve. Or, perhaps it was simply another sign of his decline.

Jess grinned. "I think that's exactly what they're talking about. Ready for another one?"

Lil's smile fell. "There's only one more."

Jess reached for the last letter in the music box. When she and Dan had finally arrived home they'd inspected the package left by Spears. The bomb squad had screened it so there was no reason to worry what might be inside. What they'd found was her mother's music box. Jess had called Lil immediately. Dan had ordered pizza and made a beer and non-alcoholic wine run.

As exhausted as she and Dan had been, they'd all enjoyed a pleasant meal together before the guys had decided to give the sisters some space. Men didn't want to be anywhere around when there were tears, and there had been plenty. No matter what else had happened today, she and Lil had needed to do this tonight.

Their mother had written letters to them. Understandably, she hadn't been able to put much of the truth in her journal or share any of it with her sister. Toward the end things had become so complicated she'd urged Wanda to stay away. Though

Helen Harris had loved her sister, it was reasonable to conclude that she'd feared Wanda's drug use would end up being a liability for her family. Anything Wanda might have overheard could have cost Lee or any one of them their life. So, she'd scared Wanda off by warning her that Lee was involved with very bad people.

The truth was, Helen and Lee Harris had both feared for their lives and the lives of their children. When he uncovered the killings taking place at the Brownfield farm, he was ordered to dig more deeply. A brief affair with Margaret Brownfield resulted in a daughter, Amanda. It was Lee's struggle with doing the right thing by all his children, including Amanda, which levied the ultimate cost.

There were still many unanswered questions, but Jess and Lil had decided that the past was right where it belonged—in the past. After tonight, the music box would be closed and locked for the last time.

Jess opened the final letter, her eyes burning with renewed emotion. The letters had been like a portal into their parents' lives. This one was dated, the day their parents died. "Okay. My turn to read, I guess."

Lil nodded. "Get it over with, I'm about cried out."

My sweet, sweet daughters,

   Each night I watch you sleep and I wonder what kind of lives you will have. I am terrified that your father and I won't be able to protect you. I wish he had never accepted this job that has cost us so very much. I was so angry with him for so long, but then I realized, he was only human. He'd made a mistake. When we married I vowed to stand by him for better or for worse. What I realized was that I loved him and the two of you too much to walk away without trying to work things out. Our family deserved a fighting chance.

Your father has decided to go to the FBI and demand protection for all of us. We made a decision that we wanted to bring Amanda with us. She is your father's child and she deserves a chance, too. Margaret has agreed to allow us to raise Amanda. She will turn State's evidence and help the authorities stop her father. She is afraid to trust anyone else so Lee and I are going to Scottsboro to pick them up. Lee wanted to go alone, but Margaret insisted that she wanted me to be there, too. I think she's scared, though I'm not sure I really trust her. The truth is, your father and I are both terrified. Unfortunately, this is the only way. The heartless people Lee works for say they cannot help us without Margaret's testimony.

I am praying the next letter I write to you will be a happier one. If not, please know that your father and I love you very much and we have tried every way we know to protect you. In the event the worst happens, I am also praying that your Aunt Wanda will be able to take care of you. Reverend Henshaw will protect these letters for you. When it's time, he'll see that you get them.

With all my love, Mom

After more tears and hugging, Lil swiped her cheeks. "Do you think Margaret Brownfield really wanted to help or do you think she's the reason they're dead?"

Jess considered the question for a bit. "Part of me believes she set them up. That she did what her father told her." She thought of Amanda's story about her mother taking her to the funeral home to say good-bye. "Except, I do think Margaret loved him—in whatever way she could. I guess we'll never know that part."

Lil tucked the final letter back into the music box and closed it. "This is all we need to know. Our parents loved us and died trying to protect us."

"That's all that matters," Jess agreed.

Lil groaned. "We should get home. I never stay up this late." She set her wine glass aside and hugged Jess. "I'll call you tomorrow. We have to get started looking for your wedding gown."

Jess shook her head. "This wedding is not supposed to be a big event. It's supposed to be a small family gathering."

"Jess." Lil took Jess's face in her hands. "Katherine Burnett has waited a long time to give her son this wedding."

"What?" Jess's jaw dropped. "He's been married three times for heaven's sake."

"And all three times the ceremonies were private little trips to the courthouse or out of the country that didn't even include his parents. Katherine needs this. They're prominent people in this town, Jess. Let her show off for goodness sake. She's gone to a whole of trouble to clear the way."

Jess rolled her eyes. "Tell me about it. I have all this paperwork to do about my one and only previous marriage and I'm not even Catholic."

"There are rules, Jess, but you don't need to worry. Katherine has everything under control. By the time she and their priest are done, you can be married in the church with the usual wedding mass, you just won't be able to receive communion when Dan does."

"How do you know all this?" Lil wasn't Catholic.

"Katherine explained everything in great detail." Lil smiled. "It's interesting."

"St. Paul's cathedral is huge. It's ostentatious. It's…" Jess groaned. "She's going to invite hundreds of people, I just know it."

"Only two fifty."

Jess's mouth gaped again. "Oh my God."

"Deep breath," Lil instructed. "Now, deal with it. I'm helping her plan this wedding. I need the practice for when Alice gets married."

"I thought this wedding was supposed to be about me and Dan."

"Ha! Make a note for future reference, sis, weddings are for the mothers. In this case, I'm standing in for mom."

Jess rolled her eyes and got up. "Come on. You need sleep. You're delirious."

Lil lifted Maddie into her arms. Jess kissed her sweet forehead. There was a lot more hugging at the door.

When Lil and Blake were on their way, Jess went back inside and crawled onto the couch. Dan and Blake had obviously worn Bear out tossing a ball to him. The pup was curled up on the rug next to the bed. Jess was pretty sure she heard him snore at least once.

Dan locked up.

"I'm exhausted just thinking about this wedding." She had made a promise to herself when she'd walked away from the showdown with Spears. From now on, she was going to have a real life— one that included more than work. But did it have to include two hundred and fifty people and a huge cathedral?

Dan sat down next to her and pulled her into his lap. "Let them have their fun. Pick out the dress and flowers you want and let them do the rest."

"And music. I'm not letting anyone else pick the music."

Dan laughed. "And the music. Mom and Dad want to make this special for us. I'm okay with it if you are."

"It's a lot of money." Jess didn't even want to think about how much.

"If it makes them happy, that's what matters."

Jess heaved a big breath. "Okay, so December 19. That will make me around five months." She groaned. "I'm going to be huge. How am I supposed to pick out a dress now when I'm continually expanding?"

Dan laughed. Jess felt the pleasant sound rumbling from his chest.

"It's not funny."

"You will be the most beautiful bride ever." He kissed her forehead. "Besides, Lil says you won't even look pregnant until you hit month six. You're so tiny a little expanding won't matter. Trust me."

"I don't believe her or you."

Dan's arms tightened around her. "I don't care how much you expand, you'll still be perfect to me."

"Whatever." She smoothed a hand over his chest. She loved this old Brighton Academy t-shirt he wore. It was more than two decades old. She remembered him wearing it back in high school. The only reason it hadn't burned in his house was because it was at his parents' house. His mom kept almost everything from the years before he left home. "Did Nancy Wolfe call about a closing date?"

"Two weeks from Monday," Dan confirmed. "Then we can start making the house our own."

"Maybe Lil and I will go over there tomorrow afternoon. She can help with paint colors." Since the house was unoccupied going in without advance notice shouldn't be an issue. The previous owner had accepted a new job in Tennessee and moved last month. He'd wanted the family settled into their new home before school started.

"We need to start shopping for furniture," Dan reminded her.

Furniture made her think of all he'd lost when his house burned. "I spoke to my realtor in Virginia.

She said I can sign a power of attorney so she can take care of the closing for me." Jess had no desire to go back there. "She'll even hire a moving company to pack up my things and ship them down here. Everything except the furniture." All the furnishings conveyed with the house. "I still have pictures and stuff from before…when we were together."

He stroked her hair, his touch making her want to wiggle even closer. "Even the locket."

"Yes." The white gold locket had been his first gift to her. He'd had their photos mounted inside and chosen a delicate matching gold chain to hold it. He'd said he wanted to be sure he was always next to her heart. "I still have the first engagement ring you gave me, too." She held out her right hand. "I could wear it on this finger." She wiggled her ring finger.

She felt his lips stretch into a smile against her forehead. "You kept it all this time."

"I kept every part of us. I boxed it up and packed it away, but I could never part with any of it."

"I did the same thing."

She leaned away from his chest so she could see his eyes. "I know. I found the pictures when I was poking around in your house."

"Sneak," he teased.

"Speaking of sneaky, what's this I hear about the possibility that you might be running for mayor?"

He laughed. "You've been talking to Gina."

Jess had checked on her at the hospital. The relentless reporter was a little bruised and battered but that hadn't stopped her from making a live appearance for the evening news from the ER.

"I did. She said Senator Baron is spearheading the effort to make it happen."

"You and I will decide if I run, when the time comes. For now, I'm more than happy being chief of police."

"Mayor Burnett." She grinned. "It has a nice ring to it."

"Mrs. Burnett is all I have on my mind right now."

"Can it really be, Dan? After all these years and all the insanity with Spears, can it finally be our time?"

He brushed his lips across hers. "Today." He kissed her again. "Tomorrow." Another, deeper kiss took her breath. "And every day after that."

Dan stripped off the t-shirt she wore and relieved her of her bra. She tugged his tee over his head and gasped at the feel of his hot skin against her breasts. He tugged her sweat pants and panties down together. She kicked free of them and then it was time to get his jeans and boxers out of the way.

He carried her to the bed and came down on top of her. Her body hummed with need. She glided her hands up his chest and around his neck. "I love you, Dan."

He kissed her nose and then her chin. "I love you."

He cupped her breast in his hand and flicked his thumb across her taunt nipple. She shivered, felt that tug of desire deep beneath her belly button.

She parted her legs and wrapped them around his, opening wider in invitation. Dan filled her in one thrust.

It didn't matter that the lights were on or that she was over forty and no longer had the perfect figure she'd had at seventeen when they made love the first time. He took his time and cherished every part of her.

She did the same, touching, tasting, taking, and giving until they collapsed together. Later, Dan whispered sweet promises to their baby.

For the first time in a long time, Jess couldn't wait for tomorrow.

CHAPTER
TWENTY-EIGHT

Jess eased out of the bed. She didn't want to wake Dan. Last night was the first good night's sleep either of them had managed in months. After the way he'd made love to her, he needed his rest.

On her way to the bathroom, she paused long enough to check her cell. Force of habit. She smiled as she read a text her ex-husband and friend had sent her last night. Gant must have brought him up to speed on the Spears situation.

Congratulations! I knew you would get that monster! I expect an invitation to the wedding, by the way.

Living in L.A., Wesley would still be sleeping at this hour. She sent a reply anyway.

Thanks. You will definitely get an invitation.

She shivered when her bladder reminded her she'd better get a move on. Having to hurry to the bathroom a dozen times a day was just another perk of being pregnant. While she sat on the toilet, Bear padded in and started licking her legs.

"I guess you have to go, too," she whispered.

He looked up at her with those big brown eyes.

"I thought so."

After she'd taken care of business, she pulled on the sweats and t-shirt Dan had slipped off her last night. She stepped into her flip-flops and grabbed the leash. As quietly as possible, which wasn't easy with Bear getting more and more excited at the prospect of going outside, she disarmed the security system and crept out the door.

At the bottom of the stairs, Jess stopped and surveyed the driveway. She smiled. It was nice not to see a BPD cruiser and two officers parked there. As grateful as she was to the department's finest, she was immensely relieved they were no longer needed. She drew in a big breath of morning air. This early was about the only time it was bearable outside during Alabama summers.

Bear tugged at the leash. She let him lead. It was so quiet. Most folks were still in bed. Who wanted to be up this early on a Saturday morning?

In a few days, it would officially be fall and eventually the weather would start to cool. Maybe after she and Dan were settled in the new house they could take a vacation. They needed a vacation. Some place far away from police work and wedding plans.

Bear left a puddle in the grass next to the driveway. Jess hoped that was all he had to do right now.

She'd forgotten to bring a bag. She was quite certain George would not be pleased if he stepped in dog poo.

George had likely heard the news about Spears and would be grateful to no longer have to deal with BPD surveillance and strange people showing up with guns. She laughed. George Louis hadn't had a clue what he was getting into when he'd offered his garage apartment to Jess.

Granted, he was one strange man, but she doubted guns and serial killers were among his life experiences until she came along.

Jess was glad their new home had already been beautifully landscaped. Unlike her landlord, she did not have a green thumb. Work around the house had never been one of her priorities.

The leash jerked free of her hold. Bear launched across the yard like a rocket.

"Bear! You come back here!" He listened like most perps did when chased. He wasn't turning around much less coming back.

Jess rushed after him. She had a feeling he was headed for that same flowerbed under the kitchen window that he loved so to scratch around in. Thank God the new property had a nice fence around the backyard. She wasn't chasing this dog on a regular basis though she probably should since she needed the workout.

"You are a bad boy." She grabbed the leash and tried to pull him away from the flowers. He was having none of it. The harder she pulled the more frantic his digging became.

"Bear," she muttered, hoping she wouldn't disturb George. He was always up bright and early. Jess doubted he wanted his morning routine interrupted by a naughty dog. "Stop digging right now."

Bear pulled something free of the dirt and mulch.

Jess stared at the thing the pup now held in his mouth.

Bone.

That couldn't be...*human?*

Jess dropped to her knees and started pushing dirt and mulch away from the base of the mound that served as a bed for the lovely flowers she and Bear were effectively destroying. Didn't matter...all she could do was dig.

Her fingers curled around an object and she pulled it loose. Her anatomy class kicked in.

*Radius...*arm bone.

"What the hell?"

Memories fired one after the other. Going into the garage below her apartment to flip a breaker, stubbing her toe on that big wooden box, and finding that silver wedding band on the floor. Her apartment being broken into. The hole in her bathroom floor that wouldn't stay filled. The missing pregnancy test. George painting over the message written on her door. Him swinging an andiron to rescue her from a killer who'd come here looking for her.

Rushing out to warn her that a stranger, a woman, walking bare foot with a gun, had gone up to her apartment.

Jess stared at the bone in her hand. She was no forensic anthropologist, but this bone didn't look as if it had been buried for very long. Had he seen Captain Allen tampering with her car and done something to protect her?

George Louis was an old man. A hermit, for the most part. He wasn't a killer.

Was he?

Jess had spent nearly two decades chasing and profiling killers. She couldn't have missed that kind of evil living right next door to her.

The creak of hinges drew her attention upward. George stood in the open doorway.

"You should come inside, Jess."

Her gaze lowered to the weapon in his hand.

For heaven's safe.

"What're you doing, George?" Next to her the puppy kept digging.

"Come inside and we'll talk," he said, his voice oddly calm.

"All right." Jess stood. She dusted off her hands and knees. "I haven't had a cup of coffee yet." Whatever was going on in that head of his, she needed to ensure he didn't get excited.

"I have decaf," he said, a note of hope infusing his tone. "Isn't that better for the baby?" He stepped back, opened the door wider for her to come inside.

Jess pushed a smile into place. Oh yes, he'd taken that pregnancy test all right. "It sure is. I'd love a cup of decaf."

George closed the door behind her, leaving Bear still digging madly. "I have your favorite blend."

"Columbian dark roast?" she asked, going for hopeful.

"Oh yes, it's very rich."

He'd been in her apartment snooping—a lot, it seemed. "I should wash my hands."

"Of course." He busied himself at the coffeepot, his attention divided between her and his preparations. "I read that during pregnancy you should wear gloves when working in the yard. It's safer that way."

"I should've thought of that." She went to the sink, not three feet from him, and turned on the water. "You think the weather's going to start cooling off?" She pumped soap into her hands and rinsed them under the running water.

While George offered his thoughts on the sort of fall they could expect, she scanned the counter for a weapon. Dammit. Why couldn't he have a knife lying handy?

Her attention lit on the stove and the cast iron skillet of bacon sizzling there. Lying next to the skillet was the fork he was using for turning the meat. Jess glanced at George then reached toward the—

"While the coffee brews, you must come see what I've done."

Jess jerked her hand back then wiped both on her t-shirt. "What have you done, George?" She felt confident they weren't talking about the same thing.

"It's a surprise." He smiled that bashful smile of his. "Just for you."

Jess glanced at the gun he still held. "We don't really need that, do we, George?" She shrugged. "It's just the two of us."

He glanced at the gun. "Don't try to fool me, Jess." His gaze leveled on hers. "I'm not nearly as naïve as you think."

"If it makes you feel more confident, then keep it." She forced her lips back into a smile. "Just be careful where you point it. We have to keep the baby safe."

He adjusted his aim ever so slightly. "Yes, of course."

"What do you want me to see, George?"

"This way." He gestured with his weapon. "It's the basement. You're going to love what I've done with it."

Hoping Dan would wake up and come looking for her, Jess walked toward the door beyond the table. She hadn't been in the basement before so she wasn't really sure if the door led to a pantry or to the basement. "Here?"

"Yes. The switch is to your right on the landing."

Jess opened the door. A short landing stood between her and a set of stairs that led into the darkness.

"Turn on the light and watch your step."

Jess flipped the switch and then grasped the railing. Taking her time, she descended into the basement. It was huge. As she reached the bottom of the stairs, she realized the main area was an almost exact replica of her apartment. Same bed, similar sofa, and tables. The little kitchen nook and closet area were the same. There were two interior doors. In her apartment there was only one that led to the bathroom.

"I worked hard to get everything right."

He ushered her toward one of the doors. When he opened it she could have been looking at her own bathroom.

"I wanted you to feel at home."

I suppose, when the time comes, you'll be moving with him.

George's words echoed in her head. He'd asked her just last week if Dan had found a new house and if she'd be moving.

I'll miss you, Jess.

She thought of all the things he'd done to make her more comfortable. The motion activated light on her landing and the porch glider she'd enjoyed so much.

Your presence makes life interesting, Chief Harris.

George Louis was lonely. He didn't want Jess to move away. She turned to him. Was that his only motive?

"You've done a wonderful job, George. I can't tell you how much safer I feel knowing you're here to take care of me."

His smile broadened as he tried to decide what to do with his free hand. "Thank you, Jess." His smile dimmed suddenly. "I'm sorry you had to find out about that terrible Captain Allen. I was only protecting you. He wanted to hurt you. I caught him in the act."

"He can't hurt me," Jess reminded him. "Because you took care of him."

George nodded. "I did. I hit him over the head with my hammer. I just kept hitting him until he stopped moving." Fury tightened his lips. "Then I dragged him into the garage and waited until I could clean up the mess."

"You cleaned it up so well no one would ever know." Jess tucked her hair behind her ear. "Allen was an arrogant bully who got what he deserved."

George laughed, the sound more like a giggle. "He wasn't so tough after I got through with him." His expression twisted into one of pure evil. "I cooked him until he was nice and tender and falling off the bone. He made the best stew and jerky. Oh and the sausage. Everybody loved it."

Bile gushed into Jess's throat. She ran for the toilet.

She gagged repeatedly, but there was nothing to throw up since she hadn't eaten.

"Are you all right, Jess?"

She wiped her mouth with the back of her hand. "Yes. Sorry." She flushed the toilet. "The morning sickness is no fun."

"Should I get you something?"

She shook her head. "The coffee will be fine."

"I forgot all about the coffee." He stepped clear of the door. "Come along and let me show you the rest, then we'll have breakfast."

Jess walked past him as she exited the bathroom. If he would just lower that weapon the tiniest bit she could try to take it away from him.

"Wait until you see what's behind door number two." He ushered her to the other door. "I was so worried when you started spending so much time at Dan's house. I thought you might not come back." He sighed. "I hope you know I was very careful when I started the fire. You were never in danger. I was watching closely."

Shock radiated through her. George had set the fire at Dan's house? "I…I'm certain you were very careful."

"Of course." He smiled, almost bouncing with excitement. "Now, close your eyes."

Jess closed her eyes and he led her through the second door. She heard the distinct sound of a light switch.

"Surprise!"

She opened her eyes and her heart lunged into her throat. Another moment was required for her brain to come to terms with what her eyes saw.

A nursery. George had created a nursery. The image of that Babies R Us packaging she'd seen in his trashcan floated before her eyes. *I'm already putting together my Christmas donation for the Children's Charity.*

Jess moistened her lips. "This is beautiful, George." She decided to go for broke. "Dan will love it, too."

George shook his head adamantly. "Dan can't be here. This is just for you and the baby. Dan was supposed to be gone by now."

Jess tensed. "I didn't know. Did he tell you he was leaving?"

"Spears did. He promised Dan would be gone. I did everything he told me to do, including taking care of that nurse. I even let him bring Nina here to stay in *your* room until he was ready for her to do her part. We had a deal. Spears said Dan would be dead and that I could have you after he was finished." George puffed out a frustrated breath. "He didn't follow through on either promise."

Her blood going cold, Jess chose her response carefully. "He did a lot of that. Eric Spears was nothing but a liar."

"He promised he would kill Dan, but he wasn't man enough to get the job done."

Jess flinched before she could school the reaction. "Dan could still go to jail for Captain Allen's murder."

"I should think so. I certainly did my part. I planted the ring and the phone. Spears had no idea I did that part. I came up with my own plan."

"Spears let you down," Jess suggested.

"He did." George stepped closer. "I know why."

"Tell me why, George?"

"He wanted you all for himself."

"I think you're right about that. He was a selfish man."

He scrubbed at his face with his free hand and adjusted his glasses. "This is his fault anyway. He made me watch you. I couldn't help myself. I watched you and I fell in love with you. He made me want you. He promised me I could have you, but he intended to take you for himself all along."

Jess manufactured a smile. "Well, he can't have me now, can he?"

"No, he can't." George smiled. "I'm going to take care of you. It was me who left your mother's music box at your door. Spears never had it. He was looking everywhere for it, but he couldn't find it. I kept it safe from him. I only told you he brought it here because I saw the news and I was worried you were out there trying to find him. I wanted to keep you safe."

How had George ended up with the music box? "How did you find it?"

"Oh, that minister came to see you. He was really worried. He left it with me to keep safe for you since you weren't home. I told Spears about his visit, but not about the music box. Spears killed him." George shook his head. "I would never kill a man of God. Spears will pay for that."

"He will," Jess agreed. She hoped he was burning in hell right this minute. Why hadn't Reverend Henshaw come to her office? He might still be alive if he had.

"You look hungry," George said, jerking her back to the present. "Come along. I smell the bacon all the way down here."

Jess climbed the stairs slowly. She prayed Dan was looking for her already. As she reached the door into the kitchen, she spotted him outside and her heart did another one of the frantic lunges. Dan was at the back door peering into the kitchen. Jess held up a hand and made a gun with her thumb and fore-finger the way kids did when they were using their imagination.

Dan backed out of view.

"Would you like eggs with your bacon?" George asked as he moved to the stove. He turned off the flame under the skillet with the bacon and reached for a nonstick pan. "I love mine scrambled. I use a little of the bacon drippings instead of butter. My sister taught me to do it that way."

Keep him distracted, Jess. "You must still miss her. Your sister, I mean."

George's expression turned cold. "Not really. Burying her lovers in the garage grew quite tedious. I can't tell you how many times I redid that concrete floor." He opened the egg carton. "She truly was a marvelous cook though."

Jess cleared the shock from her face and leaned against the counter. "I have to warn you, George. I'm a terrible cook."

With George's back to the window and door, Jess tried to see what Dan was doing but she didn't dare move in that direction.

George reached over and patted Jess on the shoulder. She jumped. "You won't have to cook. I'll do everything."

The sound of glass shattering caused George to whirl around.

Jess grabbed the skillet and swung it. Hot grease and bacon flew through the air. The handle burned her palms as the skillet connected with the back of George's head.

He hurled forward.

His weapon discharged.

Jess dropped the skillet and rammed her full body weight into him, sending him crashing to the floor.

Dan came through the door.

"Where's the gun?" Jess called out.

One, then two seconds elapsed.

"Got it."

George wasn't moving.

Jess's heart thundered so hard she could scarcely think. She couldn't get enough air into her lungs.

Dan checked George's carotid artery. "He's alive. I'll restrain him. You call 9-1-1."

Her legs wobbled when she stood. She went to the nearest landline and made the call before collapsing against the wall and then sliding down to the floor.

With George secured, Dan walked over and sat down next to her. "You okay?"

Jess nodded. "I think so." She drew in a big breath. "That's Captain Allen buried out there.

George is the one who planted the evidence against you. He's one of Spears's followers." Tears crowded at the back of her throat as she told Dan the story. She wanted to cry. She really did, but by God she was sick of tears.

"He can't hurt us now."

Jess searched his eyes and somehow managed a smile. "The way I attract sociopaths and psychopaths are you sure you want to go through with this wedding?"

Dan got to his feet and offered his hand. She put her hand in his and he helped her up. "Absolutely," he promised. "Just remind me not to buy any iron skillets."

She hugged him hard. "We have to talk about the barbecue and stew we've been eating."

Dan's face fell. "I'm not so sure I want to know."

The sound of sirens and Bear barking signaled help had arrived.

"I don't think I'll tell Harper either."

Jess walked over to where George Louis had started to squirm and moan. Envy was a powerful emotion. Men had been committing murder to get what they wanted since Cain and Abel. George had his place on the evil scale, even if he didn't look the part.

As the house filled with cops and crime scene techs, Dan's cell rang. Paramedics hefted George onto a gurney as an officer read him his rights.

"That was Harper," Dan said, putting his phone away. "He and Wells will be here in fifteen minutes.

There's been a double homicide over in Sherman Heights. SPU caught the call. You haven't even had breakfast."

Jess tiptoed and gave him a peck on the cheek. "I'll grab something to eat on the way." Right now, she had to get dressed. There were two victims waiting for her to find their killer.

At the door she glanced back at Dan and smiled.

Maybe their life together would never be normal, but this was where she belonged.

This was *home*.

ABOUT THE AUTHOR

DEBRA WEBB, born in Alabama, wrote her first story at age nine and her first romance at thirteen. It wasn't until she spent three years working for the military behind the Iron Curtain—and a five-year stint with NASA—that she realized her true calling. A collision course between suspense and romance was set. Since then she has penned more than 100 novels including her internationally bestselling Colby Agency series. Her debut novel, OBSESSION, in her romantic thriller series, the Faces of Evil, propelled Debra to the top of the bestselling charts for an unparalleled twenty-four weeks and garnered critical acclaim from reviewers and readers alike. Don't miss a single installment of this fascinating and chilling ten-book series!